Darren Carpenter is running from his love of Samuel and his future as the Coimeádaí of a Sandman.

Samuel Tolliver just wants what he wants and is willing to raise a little mischief to get it.

Dailon knows he is more than human but has no clue what he is or what he needs.

But the Fates have a plan for them, even if family, friends, and fairy royalty must get involved.

When everything goes wrong, can they make it right again?

Broken Dreams

ISBN: 978-1-4874-2315-5
Cover art by Martine Jardin

Published by eXtasy Books Inc

Look for us online at:
www.eXtasybooks.com

Broken Dreams
Broken 4

By

Deja Black

Dedication

To my readers who waited and sent me messages, thank you. I'm here, and so are my people. We are because of you.

To my editor, Debbie Nygaard, where would I be without you? You know my books better than I do, answer any question at any time, and deal with my crazy. You are the bestest!
(Yeah, I said that.)

All the love,
Deja

Chapter One

"Samuel did what?" Darren shouted, exasperated.

"You heard me, Darren," Kristoff's brandy voice, smooth and rich, sighed into the phone. The alpha mate was at the end of his rope, and Darren had joined him there years ago.

Darren didn't need this right now. His little shit was so getting it. He could practically see the handprint he would leave on Samuel's pale ass. "Another orgy?"

"Yes."

"Of humans?"

"Yes, though, it is quite ironic to hear you speak as such, as you are also human."

"I don't have time for this, Alpha Mate Kristoff. My to-do list is doubling as we speak. I know there must be more. Please continue so I can add Samuel's needs to the ones I have already." After all, it wasn't as if orgies were unfamiliar when considering his friend Samuel. Tiresome, yes. New, no.

"With my boy, I know there has to be more. It wouldn't be Samuel if there were not." Darren added one of the items he'd overlooked to the file he'd been studying earlier, then sat back to fully listen. He couldn't afford to make an error in his work merely because Samuel had gone AWOL yet again.

Kristoff's bark of laughter was loud across the phone. "You know your Samuel." He sighed. "Unfortunately, he's marked several of the humans."

"Shit," Darren groaned. He placed his head in his palm, his exhaustion suddenly overwhelming.

"Yes, complete *der'mo*, and the ice of the cake? He refuses to release them."

Darren let out a longsuffering sigh, ignoring the Russian's destruction of American slang. One week. He'd only been gone one week.

Hindsight was 20-20. What Darren needed was foresight. At the very least, he needed help. Being the one person Samuel listened to was wearing him down, no matter how he felt about the man.

Is Samuel my responsibility? So hard to answer that question.

The little witch was 23 but so fucking powerful, no one could control him. Samuel refused to listen to anyone. Not his parents, his grandfather, and barely the Alpha Mate. Darren was the only person Samuel heeded. A tired human trying to start his career, who'd had to go out of town and had no one to babysit a sex-crazed spoiled dynamo.

As a half-sprite, half-wolf, Samuel's appetite for sex was insatiable. For a human to receive his mark was almost life-threatening, because said human could then only be satisfied by the essence of the one he served. The sharing of essence between the two was particularly concerning when the one harnessing the energy had no interest in the one he'd marked.

If Samuel had marked humans, it meant he was frustrated and had allowed his feelings to control his actions. Samuel was impulsive, but he was typically careful of marks. He knew better.

It wasn't a challenge to know the true target of Samuel's rage. *Fuck, it's not my fault.*

Darren had to work. He couldn't be available to Samuel twenty-four-seven. He was determined not to live off Samuel, no matter how many times the man offered. They were friends, not lovers, though his dick got hard whenever Samuel was near him.

Darren didn't have time for relationships. He was on the path to opening a new office for his law firm and doing what he'd wanted all his life. If he could impress his bosses, he was in a prime position for success.

He was determined to be master of his own fate, subject to no one's will.

Years ago, Darren's life had nearly been forfeited. Keith Mulligan, a Sandman bent on revenge, had used him, removing the will Darren wielded like a shield. He had been nothing but a tool for the evil Keith wrought. He would never forget how Danny and Aiden, a Sandman himself, had fought to save his life. The battle, the blood, and the terror were memories that would stay with him always.

Daniel Tolliver—or as Darren preferred, Mr. T—wasn't just Samuel's teacher but had become like a father to him. Danny had surprised Darren back then. He had always been a gentle spirit, but the fierceness with which he'd fought had been impressive.

When Darren had first met Keith, the man had presented as a good guy and someone completely devoted to Danny. Keith had arrived in Danny's stead to help their play go on while Danny convalesced after an accident that put him in the hospital.

At the time, Darren had thought Keith was Danny's friend who just wanted to help. All of it was a lie. Danny had gone home to the safety of his family when he left the hospital. The only way Keith could get to Danny was through the abuse and terrorizing of Darren. That was when Darren had learned that Keith had spent years doing the same thing to Danny.

To discover that Keith was in reality a monster along with being an abuser had opened Darren's eyes to a world he hadn't known existed. His inability to see the monster for who he was made him despise himself—even more so when he discovered *what* he was.

Like Danny, Darren was a Coimeádaí, a balance for a Sandman, destined to be a mate for the same creature that tried to kill him, use him as bait and a threat. A Sandman. Darren would never forget and vowed never to be that vulnerable again.

As for Samuel, if Darren had the little minx in front of him, he wasn't sure he'd be able to deny his friend the spanking he was asking for. Had been asking for since Darren told him about his intended move. It was less than two hours away, but when Samuel's face had taken on that eerie cast, Darren knew he was in trouble.

He sighed and stretched out his long legs, enjoying the cool breeze while sitting on the hotel balcony. He was tempted to rummage through the room's bar and find something strong to take the edge off. A little burn would be just what he needed, because he was losing his fucking mind.

Darren had only spent a week in preparation for the new office and still had another week to go. There was no telling what Samuel would do with that time. Darren wasn't stupid. Samuel wanted him home, and the brat would likely do something even worse to bend Darren's resolve to move.

The thought of placing Samuel over his lap, that plump round ass at his mercy, made Darren reach for his dick. He squeezed his hefty weight, sliding his zipper down and easing his cock out. He could picture Samuel's cries when he slapped that ass to punish him. Samuel's eyes would be wet, his wet lips open in surprise, his gasps at each strike making Darren's dick leak.

"Fuck," Darren groaned. Now was not the time to think about giving Samuel what they both needed. It was up to him to keep his shit together and discern what to do so he could work without anticipating what trouble Samuel would get into . . . next.

First, though, he would give himself some relief, squeezing until his painfully hard meat spilled the cum boiling within. Then he would do his best to have a dreamless sleep, one where he didn't fear an unknown presence hovering. He would shake off the sensation that whatever waited was just around the corner. Darren would awaken fresh in the morning, and the solution would not involve giving in to fucking Samuel.

They were friends. Samuel was the only person he trusted without question. He wouldn't ruin what they had to own him. He wouldn't put their relationship in jeopardy. Not just because he'd come to value Samuel's openness, his loyalty, and his flair for all things exotic, but because he needed the man, like air to breathe. He couldn't take the chance that one day his fate would come to claim him. He wouldn't put Samuel in danger, no matter how much the man felt he could handle the world and stamp all enemies beneath his feet.

Darren never wanted to make him try.

Samuel stood in line waiting, waiting, and—*what the fuck*—waiting. He didn't have time for this shit. Darren hadn't called him yet about his latest *gasket blower,* as so colorfully described by Kristoff. So he'd marked a few humans. Had they not had the best orgasms they would ever have in their lives? Had he not fed them, spoiled them, and even taught them a little about their inhibitions? The men had none left now. They were all completely open to their sexuality. And if they felt they could only be satisfied by him because of a slip of his teeth, then it was what the Fates allowed. He would just keep telling himself that.

Okay, maybe he hadn't quite thought it through, but he was tired of Darren holding himself back from what Samuel offered him. He knew he was Darren's favorite, had been for years now. But no matter what he did to spur Darren into action, the man refused. Samuel couldn't mark Darren, and while he wanted to say it was because he hadn't tried, he had.

Sue me.

Apparently, Darren was impervious to his machinations, and that frustrated the hell out of him.

Samuel wanted more and was certain Darren did as well. They needed each other. How could he make his human realize this and mend their broken dreams?

Samuel peered around the woman in front of him, searching out the problem at the head of the line. This was one of the few coffee houses near the campus that he could walk to and not run into issues with his family. There was no way he was drinking the swill they called coffee at the campus eatery. Still, he only had ten more minutes before he would be late for class.

He stretched to see the culprit causing the delay.

What was the guy's problem? How did a person who looked like his life depended on coffee not know what he wanted?

Hell, it wasn't even like Samuel wanted to go to class. Marketing was now his third attempt at a degree. First was nursing, but that hadn't fit because of the licensing test. The NCLEX exam he would have to take to become a nurse was too intense. Then he'd switched to a teaching degree, and while he liked working with students and the psychology classes, he was not a fan of writing lesson plans. And now marketing? He needed a marketing degree for what, exactly? So he could help the alpha mate and alleviate some of his workloads?

Sure, he loved Kristoff, but ever since he'd come back from Charleston, the alpha mate had been on him to do something with himself. Why? It wasn't like he needed anything. Whatever he wanted, the pack gave him. Samuel was the alpha's grandson, he had a band he sang with, which was how he tended to pick up his little human snacks, and he was the perfect blend between a wolf and a sprite. He could wolf out if he wanted, fly if he wanted, and his powers gave him all the pleasures he ever wanted.

All except one tall, gorgeous brown man with short soft curls, who refused to bend to his will.

Stubborn ass.

Samuel's skin flushed with his frustration, and the need to cause a little mayhem was there before he realized it. Why should he deny himself? He called the wind to him, just small enough to stir up a tiny gust inside the coffee shop through the open door. Then he whispered a word soft enough it would dance in the wind and caress the time-waster's ear.

The man looked around, alarmed, and Samuel was pleased to see him order a little faster. Samuel knew the smile he wore was wicked, but with that little dip into the energy in the room, he was eager for just a little more.

Samuel raised his hand, wondering what would happen if he fed a little of his hunger into the small shop, a little of the need that beat against his psyche. No matter how many he fucked—wolves, humans, witches, or other paranormals—none were enough when he truly wanted Darren.

Someone should be happy. Why not the people in here at 9 o-fucking-clock in the morning? Many of the customers probably came from campus and possibly were just as fed up as he was with the whole higher education process. He was certain they didn't want to be up this early. He knew *he* didn't.

He raised his arms, only to have them snatched just as quickly from the air.

"That's enough, don't you think?" a deep voice inquired behind him.

Power thrummed along Samuel's wrists as his arms were brought down and he was firmly captured. "The fuck."

"Shh, now. Let's not cause a scene, at least not the one you seemed to be going for. I have places to go, too, so I let you have your fun with hurrying that gentleman along. But now you just want to cause trouble."

Samuel growled when he was pulled back against a solid wall of flesh. He yanked to get free, but the man who held him was stronger than expected. A paranormal?

"Let me go," Samuel rasped.

"Not until you promise to be a good boy and leave the little humans alone."

"You can't make me."

"Oh, my darling. You have no idea what I can and will do. Now, let's not try me, hmm?"

Samuel's curiosity was piqued. Who was this asshole, and why did being a good boy thrill him in a way he hadn't felt since he'd last sat on Darren's lap in the safety of his big arms?

Samuel banked the magic he'd been prepared to gift the people who would have benefited from a little break in the monotony.

"Fine," he ground out, adding a little pout to his lips.

"See. That wasn't hard, was it? Now, I'll let your arms go, and you and I will wait patiently in the line. We'll order coffee and have a seat outside."

Samuel's arms were released, but the energy that had singed his skin remained. He turned then and realized he was standing next to Dr. Dailon Walker.

Dr. Walker was taller than Samuel, but then most men were. At 5'8, Samuel was one of the shorter members of the Iroquois Pack. But what he lacked in height, he made up for in stature. Being able to release wings from his back at a whim did that for a person. Still, the way Dr. Walker towered over him was exciting, and the hum of dark energy surrounding the man made Samuel's mouth water.

Samuel stared into eyes that appeared to be mercurial, blending from blue to green to a golden red that reminded him of burnished autumn leaves.

"Stop staring, little one. We don't want to draw attention

now, do we?"

If the way the professor had grabbed his arms before hadn't made them a focal point, what else could? And he didn't miss the slight curve to the professor's lips, indicating his amusement.

"Well, we could. I don't have a problem being the center of attention."

"No, but I do. So turn around and give the coffee barista your order. I'm paying."

"I don't need you to pay for me." That didn't mean he wasn't a little pleased with the offer. He enjoyed being cared for, the center of someone's attention. If not Darren, why not the professor?

"I won't start with what you need, and I'm not asking. Your order, please." Dr. Walker turned Samuel around by wrapping a large hand firmly around his wrist.

There was something about the young man that had made Dailon take over. The moment he entered the coffee shop, he'd felt the energy rolling off of Samuel. The young man was Dr. Ali Marshall's favorite student, one he favored because there was so much more to the beautiful boy than he was displaying. Ali and Dailon taught many of the same classes. Yet where Dailon leaned more toward general ethics, coupled with business, Ali preferred medical ethics, which worked out for both.

Dailon liked studying people and unearthing their beliefs. Their moral core had always entertained him. His mothers had approved of his choice when he'd approached them with the idea of teaching years ago. They had agreed it was a field he would do well in, as he was ever inquisitive of human nature.

As witches, his mothers understood his needs and

encouraged him to explore whatever fed his thirst to learn. Knowing the why of human action fascinated him. Had for many years. He still had questions about human motivation. Not human himself, he found the reasons behind actions enthralling.

So here he stood, having captured a mystery he'd observed in Ali's classes, had desired in a way that would probably frighten many. There was a time when Dailon would have avoided this, would have backed away from the darkness in his mind, the thoughts that made him wish for things he shouldn't. But the longer he lived, the more he wanted. It had become a need he couldn't outrun.

This beautiful boy with alabaster skin and a riotous head of fiery hair asked questions others were afraid to ask. Challenged everyone around him. Ali was right. Samuel Tolliver was brilliant, but he was also other. Dailon could sense it, wanted to taste it. And then to have witnessed him playing with the humans so recklessly? Samuel needed a keeper.

Instead of letting Samuel wreak havoc, he'd grasped those thin muscular arms and nulled his energy, which had thrown Samuel off balance. He wasn't sure where his abilities originated, but his mothers had helped teach him to control them.

He had them to thank for a normal life, one that could have been far different if he'd appeared on any other person's doorstep in the middle of the night more than thirty years ago. Instead, the Fates allowed him to find the two women who loved him and reared him as their very own. His mothers were eccentric, colorful, spirited, and bold. And loved him without fail.

His existence was a mystery, one easily overlooked by his mothers. But trying to unravel the puzzle for himself left him lost and alone at times.

Were there others like him? Those who could visit the world of dreams and struggled with the darkness within? Did he struggle with the darkness? Or had he fallen completely? The thoughts he was having about Samuel Tolliver, the things he wanted to do to him, were not the things of brightness.

He wanted to make Samuel cry with pleasured pain and wanted to taste his blood. He wondered what Samuel's dreams would be like.

Dailon brought Samuel closer to him, inhaling his sweet scent. He should be ashamed of himself. He should be trying to protect Samuel, but he was far more fascinated by what Samuel would sound like when he screamed.

Now, now. What was happening here?

Samuel was not one to be cowed by anyone. This felt different, though. He had allowed Dr. Walker to dominate him. Almost craved it. While he could wolf out with the best of them, he lacked the whole *find a mate for life* thing his father had. He knew who he was and what he wanted, no matter the form he took.

But . . .

He wasn't one to ignore the possibility of a forever. He'd thought it was Darren, still wanted it to be. Yet Dr. Walker was an anomaly that couldn't be ignored. Samuel wanted to see more.

How many times had someone demanded his attention, commanded it? With his being smaller, slighter than those deemed more powerful, he was treated gently, as if he wasn't a danger. That was typically when the need to show his fangs appeared, and he acted. The results could be a public orgy, a tornado of butterflies at his command, or flying across a stage with an audience who thought his wings were part of the props.

But here was Dr. Walker telling him to be good. As if he knew exactly what Samuel was capable of, what he could do with just a crook of his finger.

It was thrilling.

It seemed Dr. Walker saw Samuel beneath the surface, and he wasn't afraid. That was the other piece to the puzzle for Samuel. Once he revealed his true self, others backed away.

Not Darren. Never Darren. His best friend loved him, and he knew that without question. But the love Darren had for him was all wrapped up in some stupid need to protect him like he couldn't protect himself. He waited for the day Darren finally realized they were meant to be together, and no matter how much Darren tried to avoid his fears, they would be . . . one day.

For now, though, Samuel would see just what Dr. Walker had in mind.

Chapter Two

The phone rang a fourth time, and Darren didn't like it. Samuel never let a call ring more than twice, no matter what he was doing. Maybe it was hypocritical, but Darren liked being Samuel's priority.

What was he up to? Where was he?

It was almost ten in the morning, time for Samuel's first class of the week. Yes, he knew Samuel's schedule and had helped him choose his classes, even though he still felt like majoring in business was not what Samuel wanted to do. Still, he knew every class and every teacher.

Anything that involved Samuel is mine to know.

When the phone nearly rang a fifth time, Darren was looking for his keys.

"Hello," a deep voice answered.

The sound instantly had Darren's balls aching. Simultaneously his body was on fire, and he became a man thirsting for a drink. He hated not being in control of himself, especially his reactions to unknown stimuli.

"Darren, I presume," the voice continued.

No one answered Samuel's phone. Or no one had before. Samuel kept it close to him, was quite territorial of the device. Darren fell into the stool in front of the kitchen island, keys gripped tightly in his fist.

"Yes, where's Samuel?" He took a breath but tried to keep it quiet. He didn't want to give away anything.

"Samuel is finishing his coffee before he heads to class."

Coffee? Had this person and Samuel been together. Samuel

always refused to keep his playthings overnight.

Who was this person? Why is he answering Samuel's phone?

"Let me speak to him," Darren added steel to his words, using the tone that typically had others jumping to do his bidding.

"No." Calm and controlled, the response was unexpected.

The man's tone was so unlike how Darren felt. *Who the hell is this guy?*

Everyone who knew Samuel and Darren knew how much they were a unit. Samuel was his. Maybe not the way he wanted him, but the way they needed to be.

"What do you mean *no*?" The steel became ice, and Darren stood.

"I mean you have things to do, Darren. Things that require your attention, and Samuel's tantrum doesn't need to distract you. I will take care of him, and when you return, you can take over as per usual."

"Who is this?" Yes, Darren had been frustrated that he had to deal with Samuel alone while he had things to do, important things that would help further his career. But he was used to Samuel, used to being summoned by his family. He was used to being Samuel's rock, and here was this person, this unknown, trying to take that away from him?

"Dr. Dailon Walker. I'm one of the professors at the university here. I saw your Samuel preparing to cause mayhem."

Fuck! What had Samuel done that he was able to draw this professor's attention? More importantly, what would the pack do if they discovered this latest mishap?

"Mayhem?" Samuel questioned in the background with a laugh.

Darren sighed. There was his sneaky little one. There was only so much he could do miles away. And knowing Samuel, there was nothing the minx wouldn't do to make sure Darren got his ass home. This could all be a warped plan of Samuel's, and Darren could be falling for it. It changed nothing.

"What happened?" he asked Dr. Walker.

"He felt things weren't moving quite fast enough for him. It wasn't enough to help the confused coffee drinker at the head of the line speed up his order. He wanted to shake things up a bit. Fortunately, I was there to stop that from happening."

Darren sighed again. He didn't know this Dr. Walker person, but he had to admit he was grateful. "Thank you."

"It was no trouble. I enjoy seeing what he will do next, within reason."

There was heat in the stranger's voice now, anticipation that curled itself around Darren's balls and squeezed. Darren suddenly wanted to see Dr. Walker. Samuel, too.

"He's a good person." He felt the need to defend Samuel.

Too often, people didn't understand that Samuel was a giver. Sure, he rejoiced in causing chaos—he was a menace—but he was always there for his family when they needed him. He also volunteered in the human world, a world he seemed to feel suited him more than his pack, and participated in charities.

His fiery hair and wicked tongue made a person think twice about approaching him. When they did, he wrapped himself around them and drank them in, discarding them if he found them unworthy. Still, he had a heart that shined, and Darren loved to watch it glow.

"Of this, I have no doubt, but he bears watching, something you can't do alone. Aren't you tired of being alone, Darren?"

Dr. Walker's voice bore a hint of knowing, as though he was aware of the ache within Darren. The struggle to understand this person and how he was suddenly entangled in their lives twisted Darren's thoughts. He'd hidden his frustrations from everyone else so long, including Samuel, and here was this man he barely knew diving beneath the surface.

A moan tried to escape from behind his teeth. Yes, he was

tired of being alone, of not having Samuel the way he wanted, of always being the rescuer and not the taker.

Can I have that? Would it even be fair?

Darren had a destiny, one that wouldn't allow him to have Samuel the way he wanted. Hell, he couldn't have anyone for himself. The best he could hope for was friendship. That had to be enough.

I'm a Coimeádaí, a human meant to be the mate of a Sandman.

When he was little, the only Sandman he'd heard of was a song his grandmother sang. Then as a high school student, he met one. Keith, the evil asshole that had tried to use him, bleed him, and keep him as a souvenir.

For some reason, as a Coimeádaí, Darren was considered a blessing, a person who could help balance the power of a creature that lived multiple lifetimes. He'd learned from Aiden that darkness followed a Sandman. The power often used to bring peace, help promote change, and save others as they passed from one journey to another could become twisted, manipulating the Sandman. Without a Coimeádaí, the Sandman emerged fully into a creature of fear and terror—one who controlled the dreamer, causing disorder and chaos, ruined lives, and fed evil.

How could Darren hope to overcome an outcome one Sandman embraced and another feared? Aiden had given up on the light, and from what Danny had said, was on a path to invisibility, his spirit changing so drastically as he began to surrender. Alone so long, Aiden had given up on ever having a mate.

When Aiden met Danny, he hadn't known what to do. Suddenly his dreams were being realized. And yet? He had been afraid.

Not so for Keith. No, that bastard had wanted to live, and he had no qualms about abusing lives to maintain his goal. First Danny and then Darren.

Fortunately, Keith had not succeeded. Darren and Danny

had survived, and Aiden accepted what Danny was to him. He treasured it. But they had all gone through so much. Too much.

Darren vowed to never face that again. He couldn't.

Until now, he'd been alone in his fear, kept himself from falling too hard for Samuel, from wanting more. And here was this stranger, Dr. Walker, asking him for answers he'd hidden from everyone.

He didn't know this. He should just say no and tell this Dr. Walker to hand Samuel the phone.

"Sometimes." He shocked himself as the truth slipped out.

It was hard sometimes, to be the human friend of a being so beautiful and yet so deadly that others feared him. It was even harder striving for more as a black male in a world where opportunities were as elusive as tanzanite, the ability to attain power after having struggled for years. There were so many strikes against him, but his grandmother had never allowed him to limit himself. It wasn't easy. The haters were out there and the doubters, too. There were so many traps set for a man like him—black, out, and refusing to back down—so many places he wasn't welcome.

Darren had fought tooth and nail to be where he was. And the opportunity to work for one of the premier law firms in Louisville, Kentucky, was no easy feat. The chance to open a new office? It was everything he'd wanted.

But not everything, right?

He was driven, but he was also lonely. He wanted someone in his bed at night who welcomed him home. He wanted Samuel, and not just as a friend. Fuck, being a couple of hours away made the ache more acute, more painful.

"See, how hard was that?" Dr. Walker's smooth voice snapped reality back into place. "Now, I'm going to take Samuel to class. He may say hello, and then he'll hang up so you can do what you need. You're no longer alone, Darren Carpenter. I'm here to help." It was soothing, the words. Both comforting and strong.

And surprisingly, Darren was grateful.

"Who are you?" Darren asked. Or *what are you?*

"For now, a friend. Someone who wants to help. Later, we'll see."

Darren couldn't see the smile, but he could hear it in the man's words. The innuendo there caused him to lick his lips nervously.

Darren heard the phone change hands.

"Darren," Samuel said, obviously flustered as well. "I'm going to head to class now. If you want to talk later, I'd like that, but I'll try to understand if you can't."

"You will?" Darren questioned. He was shocked, to say the least, but he'd be lying to himself if he said he wasn't a little relieved. No guilt trip. No tension. Just he'd understand.

Darren nodded though Samuel couldn't see him. He could get behind that.

"You know I can't go to sleep without talking to you, baby. I'll call later. Promise." He went for calm and encouraging. If Samuel was a good headspace, he wanted him to remain there.

"You fucking . . ." Samuel ground out.

He must have moved away from the phone because the rustling sound Darren heard was followed by a mumbled admonishment.

Then Samuel was back, clearing his throat uncomfortably. "So, no one's perfect. I said I would try. But, yes, tonight. That would be great." This obviously came through gritted teeth, but he'd said the words, and that was further than they'd ever been before.

"Okay, have a great class," Darren soothed.

"I will. Talk to you later," Samuel answered.

Darren heard a sigh and then what sounded like a kiss. It wasn't like Samuel was a virgin. His boy got around . . . often.

Darren learned not to let it bother him. After all, he wasn't a virgin either. But Darren would have given anything to see the man kissing Samuel. To be there to witness it for himself. His dick was hard from imagining it.

That was new, the desire to watch. He'd never felt that before.

What the hell is happening with me?

Maybe he was horny. It had been a while since he'd been with anyone. Perhaps the absence of a tight ass wrapped around his thick width was playing tricks on his mind.

Still?

Trying to visualize the stranger who seemed to calm his Samuel in mere minutes was an image he couldn't resist. He pictured dark hair, green eyes, and a wide body. It wasn't what he typically went for. Often, he chose a tight, compact frame, someone he could bend to his will. Someone with red hair, sometimes blond. Someone like Samuel.

Samuel was both lithe and muscular, his slim frame deceptively strong.

There were times when strangers failed to realize just how strong Samuel was. They were quickly destroyed or eaten alive. Samuel could enthrall with a word, devour sexual essence pulsing from a body, and play nature like his own symphony. And yet, he'd given in to this man.

Dr. Walker was not to be underestimated. Darren was interested in seeing what made him someone who could tame Samuel's beast.

"Darren," Dr. Walker questioned.

"Yes." Darren had tuned out for a bit and had no idea how many times his name had been called.

"I have a class myself. So, after I deliver Samuel to his classroom, I have to run. I'm sure you have questions. So, let's chat later, hm?"

"Oh, yes. Certainly." *Do I sound breathless? I hope not.*

"Good. I'd like that. Samuel is an interesting man, and as

you two are so close, I would love the opportunity to get to know you both."

The suggestive tone did nothing to alleviate the tightness of Darren's pants. If anything, they only became that much more restrictive as his length fought for release.

"I agree. That would be nice." *Better than nice.*

"Good. I have your number. We'll talk later, perhaps when Samuel and I have dinner."

"Dinner?"

He heard the same echo from Samuel.

"Yes, it is typically how one gets to know others. Until later, Darren."

The phone went dead, and Darren was left looking at the silent rectangle in his hand. The conversation had been both surreal and thought-provoking. It had also left him horny as hell.

Chapter Three

This was not a world he would ever have envisioned for himself. Samuel looked at the man beside him, strolling carelessly like there were no burdens he had to bear. Dr. Walker was an enigma, and that had to be why Samuel's wolf was interested, why he felt the need to be closer, to listen to him. To allow him to admonish him.

Nobody puts Baby in the corner.

"What are you?" Samuel growled as Dr. Walker guided him across the street on his way to the education building, his hand on the small of Samuel's back. The day had turned out to be a promising one, with the sun shining, the earlier clouds having dissipated. It was as if the weather were reflecting Samuel's anticipation.

"Careful, I promised Darren to keep you safe," Dr. Walker warned, capturing his elbow to pull him back.

Oh, that van would not have hit me. Samuel was entirely too swift for some tanker wannabe to take him out. Use the wind, and he could flit across in no time. Well, he could if his elbow wasn't currently in a firm hold. Samuel had to admit he didn't want that hand to let go. The warmth of the professor's touch, coupled with his take-charge air, made him shiver.

Not wanting to give himself away, he said, "You did not," and snorted. Still, he allowed Dr. Walker to maneuver him into a corner of the building.

"He believes in me. That's what matters. You matter a great deal to Darren, and I can understand why."

Whiskey brown eyes stared at Samuel as the hand at his

back slipped around, pulling him closer. He pressed his hands against the professor's chest, enjoying the feeling of the hard body against his.

Samuel glanced around. People were walking in a hurry to get somewhere. There was a delivery truck with a guy sitting inside having the conversation from hell on his phone, if his gestures and the artfully styled swearwords were anything to go by. The guy looked familiar, but Samuel didn't waste his thoughts on him. He was more interested in being trapped in the corner of a building by a tall professor with beautiful eyes that nearly glowed staring him down, their bodies flush against each other, with the professor's dick making an impression against Samuel's belly.

"We're out here in front of everyone. I just met you. You might see someone you work with. I'm a student. None of this bothering you?" Samuel questioned, listing the reasons why this should bother the man.

"One, people should mind their own business. Two, I can make this a memory for all involved. Three, I'd rather see what the inside of your mouth tastes like." All of this was said as the professor drew closer, the heat from his words skimming over Samuel's flesh.

The kiss wasn't sweet or tender. It was brutal and taking, Dr. Walker's grip on him tight as he slammed against Samuel. When a person kissed Samuel, especially the first time, it was a gentle peck, a little get-to-know-me kiss. This was heat and fire. And when Dr. Walker slid his finger down the tight line of Samuel's jeans as if searching for his hole, Samuel nearly made the job easier by reaching to pull down his pants.

He burned with want. The desire to have his hole filled by what the professor was offering overwhelming his senses.

Dr. Walker rose up then, and his smile was pure darkness, his lips puffy from the kiss they shared. "I could do anything I want to you right here. Fuck you hard and deep against this wall, fill your hole full of my seed, and savor your scream." He licked Samuel's throat before biting him sharply. "I would love to hear you scream, Samuel. But now is not the time. Right now, you have class. Your professor is a friend of mine, and I would rather not be the reason you're late to class. Tell him hello for me. And be good."

He bent for another kiss, this time biting Samuel's bottom lip hard enough to draw blood. When he lifted his mouth, Samuel watched him lick away the red from his own lips. Samuel pressed a hand against the assaulted place the professor left behind. He touched his tongue to it and groaned when his dick hardened, wanting more.

"What are you?" Samuel asked, dazed.

Dr. Walker smiled and opened the door. "Go to class, Samuel. Don't forget to talk to Darren. No guilt trips or threats. Don't make it easy for me to punish that sweet ass of yours."

Samuel was nudged inside, but he didn't go willingly. He watched Dr. Walker walk away, his hand pressed against his lips, savoring the feeling.

When he could no longer see the man, he turned to go up the stairs, down the hall, and into his class.

Samuel couldn't say what the class covered that day or that he even cared. The only thing he could think about was Dr. Walker kissing him, then licking the blood from his lips. He wanted to show Darren, share it with him, and have him kiss it and make it better. Instead, he would wait, be patient, for once. Darren had work to do, a life to prepare for, and maybe Samuel needed to do a better job of remembering that.

When the class was over, Samuel remained in his seat, replaying the events prior. He took a breath and looked up to see Dr. Marshall gathering his things. Dr. Marshall was a tall man with broad shoulders who had a penchant for brightly colored suits that he often paired with even brighter shirts and socks. Samuel loved the old man with his wry sense of humor and keen eye. The fact that he and Dr. Walker were friends when the two were so far apart in age was a mystery to him, but then time was sometimes irrelevant. Relationships were what mattered.

Dr. Marshall glanced up from packing and raised a wiry brow. He'd recently shaved his head, the gleam from the overhead lights distracting Samuel for a moment.

"Tolliver?" he called from his desk, clicking a button to turn off the projector for the day's lesson.

"Sir," he responded, certain he sounded just as unsure as he felt.

"You all right, young man? You're typically one of the first out of here as soon as class is over." He sounded worried, and that was nice.

Dr. Marshall wasn't one of those people who looked at Samuel as if he were weak. The professor seemed to respect his opinions, often inviting him to participate in discussions in class. Even if this wasn't exactly a calling for him, he liked the man well enough to try.

"I'm fine. Just a lot on my brain right now, projects and all."

And all? Like that had even been a consideration.

He was thinking of the man who'd shaken his world with a kiss. And had occupied his brain for the hour since being left at the door. Samuel couldn't wait to speak to Darren, to tell him about Dr. Walker. Maybe it would make Darren jealous enough to growl the only way his human could and then become all possessive, the way Samuel liked him.

Remembering Dr. Walker's request, he said, "Uh, Dr. Walker told me to tell you hi."

Dr. Marshall's eyes rose. "He did, hm?" He gathered his materials and pulled his messenger bag over his shoulder, then slowly moved toward Samuel. "You have a nice talk?"

Odd question. Samuel grinned, certain the look was perfect because Dr. Marshall blinked hard for a moment. "Maybe?" *What's going on here?* "Why?"

"Well, to be honest, he and I have discussed you before. How brilliant a mind you have for someone so young. He's mentioned wanting to meet you." Dr. Marshall shrugged guiltily. "I figured why not. I've never seen two people who needed to meet more. You could do with a little . . . Uhm . . ."

Samuel stood, observing the way Dr. Marshall stepped back to give him room. He inhaled. Nothing. There was nothing at all. Not even fear. "I could do with a little what, Dr. Marshall?"

Dr. Marshall cleared his throat roughly. "Direction, Mr. Tolliver. When I look at you, I see potential. I see a young man who could do so much more than what you're doing right now. You cannot be a career student, Samuel, when there is a world waiting on you to contribute." He pulled his glasses off, wiped them quickly, and placed them on.

Samuel was shocked. That wasn't the answer he had expected at all. No one expected anything of him. He was the troublemaker, the shirker, that *boy*, as called by many, but no one expected anything good from him. Certainly not for him to contribute to the world.

"You do?" Samuel crossed his arms as if daring Dr. Marshall to say it was a lie.

"I do, Mr. Tolliver. There's no question you can't answer in this class, no matter how you pretend indifference. You could practically teach this subject if you wanted. But I never see you with anyone, no friends or conversation after class. I've heard a few tales in passing of your conquests and the rumors of what one of your local music concerts can become, but that's it. I believe there's more. Dr. Walker agreed, and he's never one to mention things haphazardly."

Samuel let that sink in and smiled tentatively. "No one has ever said anything like that to me." He took a deep breath.

"I'm heading out. Is there anything I can help you with, Dr. Marshall?"

"No, Mr. Tolliver. I'm fine. Could use a TA one day, though. Perhaps you might consider that?"

Samuel nodded as his face heated. "I'm not making any promises."

"Of course not." Dr. Marshall smiled. "But it wouldn't hurt to look into."

Samuel shrugged and turned away.

"Look into it, Mr. Tolliver. Another semester, and the position could be yours," Dr. Marshall called behind him.

"I'll think about it, Dr. Marshall," Samuel called back.

And maybe he would.

Samuel had had the weirdest day ever. It was official. First, Dr. Walker, who the very thought of made him ache to be filled in places he never shared with anyone. He was the aggressor, felt he had to be. It was his way. But Dr. Walker took, and Samuel had loved every moment of it.

Dr. Walker hadn't treated Samuel like he was lesser. Instead, he'd manhandled him as if he could take it, and he wanted more. He was hungry for it.

Pain? Samuel didn't mind it. He craved it. He'd pictured his ass reddened by Darren's powerful hand and had often pushed him with the hope that Darren's incredible control would finally snap. Perhaps he didn't have to do it alone anymore. The way Dr. Walker had talked to Darren, Samuel could almost feel Darren's interest over the phone.

And now? Dr. Marshall was asking him to consider applying for a TA position. Him. Samuel Tolliver, wayward child of Conner and Shelly Tolliver. The one people made excuses for rather than expectations.

Mind blown.

What did Samuel do with that?

Chapter Four

"Samuel," a voice called, one Samuel's cock recognized immediately. His body thrummed with energy that begged to be released. He was a tightrope walker desperately trying to remain calm before he found himself memorialized on the floor below.

His wolf stirred, sniffing about. It stretched and preened, eager to catch the attention of the man before him. Dr. Walker casually leaned against a tree, cool and carefree, his muscular arms folded against his wide chest.

Samuel wanted to lick him. Now.

"Are you following me?" Samuel asked as he faced the man of his most recent fantasies.

Dr. Walker's smile was slow, the heat of interest sparkling in his swirling eyes. Samuel lost himself for a moment, transfixed by the multihued shades of blue and gold as they spun and danced.

"No, why would I do that when I could simply wait? This is where I dropped you off, of course." He offered an arm to Samuel. "Come with me."

"What if I don't want to?" Samuel hoped his eagerness to do whatever this man said was less apparent than he thought.

"One of the things Dr. Marshall admires about you, Samuel, is your honesty. Why change that now? We both know you want to. Now, come, or would you like me to make you? The idea of you under my control tempts me to do things that would leave the most beautiful bruises on that pale skin of yours. Here, beautiful one." The last was a demand.

A demand Samuel found himself helpless to ignore. The professor was right. He wanted . . . wanted so much it scared him. He had to clamp his teeth against asking for those promised bruises on his flesh. *Shit. This is surreal.*

Dr. Walker was sexy as hell, with dark hair so thick Samuel could picture gripping it while they enjoyed each other. There was a shock of gray at his right temple, which only made him want the man more. The professor was taller than him, not towering, but he sensed Dr. Walker could easily pick him up if he wanted.

Darren was taller than them both with a build most wolves had, solid and rangy. Growing up on pack lands might have something to do with that. He was younger than Dr. Walker but older than Samuel.

Samuel tried to picture Darren standing side by side with Dr. Walker, the two of them ready to use him. *My Double Ds.* He smiled at his new nickname for the pair and ran his tongue along his lips. Then he took Dr. Walker's arm and was immediately drawn to the man's side.

"Naughty thoughts there, Samuel?" Dr. Walker asked.

Not for the first time, Samuel had to wonder if the man could read his mind. He had no idea what Dr. Walker was, but whatever creature lay beneath his human exterior, Samuel sensed it was both deadly and dangerous.

And Samuel liked that idea very much.

"I'll never tell." And yes, he added a flirty note.

"It's a good thing you don't have to. You're finished with classes for the day. I'd like to take you home," Dr. Walker said, keeping him close.

"I typically just call someone to pick me up." It was one of his concessions to the pack, or more importantly, to Kristoff.

The alpha mate had decided if Samuel arrived at school with a packmate and returned with a packmate, there would be no worries of him causing trouble. Unfortunately for them, he often ditched the selected guardian for the day and sought out his entertainment.

Before meeting Dr. Walker, Samuel had decided to drop by a club and work off his frustration.

But home alone with the professor is more appealing.

Samuel tried to picture Dr. Walker in his house. Though he could be accused of being scatterbrained, his home was organized, with every item having a proper place. It was his sanctuary where he could avoid judgment. He had brought his hookups there because he could control them, feed on them without interruption. Sure, Alpha Mate Kristoff visited occasionally, but he was the only one who would chance running into a plaything. After Samuel's last guest had become enthralled, he hadn't invited anyone over, choosing to see his hookups in a room or sometimes their place.

Still, Dr. Walker wasn't a hookup, and he wasn't the alpha mate. Samuel looked forward to seeing the man in his home.

Mmm, Alpha Mate Kristoff. He and Samuel's grandfather, Alpha Jeremiah Tolliver, had finally claimed each other. It had taken years for his grandfather to get the stick out of his ass and realize the jewel he had in Kristoff Dumanovsky. It was a shame Samuel only saw the man as family now. In the past, he would have loved an opportunity to see exactly what drove his grandfather crazy. Kristoff was a feast for the senses, but from the moment Samuel had met Darren, the human had been it for him.

Sure, he'd sampled an ass now and then, shoved his dick into a tight waiting throat when available, and fed his energy whenever the need was too great to be ignored. But they were only placeholders. How many times had he dreamed of Darren demanding him to end it, telling him that he was his alone?

Darren was determined to keep Samuel safe from the possibility of a Sandman taking him and leaving Samuel in the cold.

Like that would ever happen.

But there was no way he could convince his Darren of that.

Samuel had heard the stories of Keith and what he'd done to Darren. If he had known Darren then, there was nothing he wouldn't have done to protect him. He would have given anything to keep Darren safe, to never have him face the thing that still gave him nightmares where he woke in a cold sweat and pulled Samuel close on nights when they slept together. Samuel knew when Darren needed him, and he refused to let the man fight his fears alone anymore.

Samuel cherished the nights he and Darren spent together, but sleep was all they did. Samuel had always left wanting more.

And now?

Samuel looked up at Dr. Walker as the man strode forward and wrapped an arm around him possessively.

Now, he wanted this man and Darren. Why couldn't he have both?

There had to be a reason he felt safe with this man, why his wolf thudded against the cage of his mind. He wasn't alone in this. Just as his beast had identified Darren as his, it also recognized its mate in Dr. Walker.

"You're quiet. I feel that's an anomaly." Dr. Walker stopped then and pulled Samuel closer.

Any closer and Samuel might be able to throw his legs around Dr. Walker's hips. He'd love to have the man hold him tightly against that delicious frame of his.

"No, just nothing to say." He smiled innocently, or at least tried for innocence. It wasn't as if he had deep ties with what that might be like. Neither he nor his siblings were innocent for long with the way their blood had sped their growth.

Dr. Walker looked at him, one dark brow raised in question. "Hm. How was Dr. Marshall's class today?" he asked as they strolled toward the parking lot.

"It was fine." Taking a moment, he messaged today's

driver that he had a ride and promised to head home. No one needed to worry. Yes, he would contact Kristoff the moment he got in. Done with promises he would keep or not depending on what the professor wanted, he put away his phone.

"Really? What did he cover? I love my friend, but his class can be a bore at times. The only thing of interest in his class he ever shared with me was when you showed up there. I think he did it on purpose." Dr. Walker bent and kissed him.

"On purpose?" Samuel said on a moan.

"Yes. Let's take the elevator to the second floor, faculty parking."

Samuel sighed as Dr. Walker's hand slid down the curve of his ass.

"An elevator?"

"Yes, little one. No worries. I won't fuck you in it . . . yet. I'd rather Darren hears how lovely you cry with my dick in your ass. The elevator is close to where my car is parked, and I'm more interested in spending time with you. The elevator gets us there faster." He kissed him again, and Samuel realized how much he enjoyed being kissed.

"Okay," Samuel's answer was barely a whisper.

"Now, you asked about Dr. Marshall's purpose. Dr. Marshall and I have been friends for many years. As with any person who becomes my friend, he realizes that I'm not quite the same as the humans he knows." The doors opened, and they stepped on, hand in hand.

"Humans?"

"Yes, you see, I'm not human, as you may have guessed. What I am exactly, I'm not truly certain. I know possibilities from what I've read, but as long as I have known myself, I have never known what I am."

This day just keeps getting stranger.

The ride in the elevator was tame, with Dr. Walker's proprietary hand caressing Samuel's ass. They didn't speak, just waited for the ride to end. He wanted to know more, but now was not the time to push. He waited. He was getting better at it.

When they arrived at Dr. Walker's car, Samuel was surprised to see a black Subaru with wicked curves and an aerodynamic frame that he knew could hug the road. His fingers were itching to try. It wasn't a Lexus, a Mercedes, or even a Tesla as he would have expected a man like Dr. Walker to drive, but he'd bet it purred. Hell, it probably even roared. It seemed every professor on the campus wanted to prove how much money they had and poured every dime of it into a car to validate them. Boring cars just like everyone else's. Obviously, Dr. Walker was different.

Samuel smiled and savored another gentle kiss Dr. Walker placed on his lips.

"Samuel, meet my Darlene. She's my baby." His voice felt like a caress.

Samuel shivered, wanting to hear that voice for other things, too.

Like, night-time things.

In bed things.

On the wall things.

On the floor things.

Was this too fast? This desire overriding his senses? Samuel was used to moving quickly, but it had never been quite this intense. And when had he started questioning himself? His pace? That wasn't like him.

Maybe I should take a step back? Take a moment to think?

"Samuel, darling. What's on your mind?"

Dr. Walker's hand was cool against his face, tiny flicks of electricity dancing along his skin.

"Look at your eyes, so beautiful. They reflect those chaotic thoughts dancing around behind them." Dr. Walker's cool lips touched his cheek, and his hand fell away.

"I believe you were going to take me home?" Samuel

asked, his heart racing.

Am I running away? That's not me. But this is different. I need a moment.

Time.

Dr. Walker nodded. "Yes, of course. Bending you over Darlene right now and sliding my cock into your ass is not on the table, no matter how lovely you look." He nodded, happy with his decision. "Okay, let's go before I don't give a fuck."

Samuel laughed, light and happy. His insides glowed with warmth.

Who is this man?

And what the hell is he doing with me?

Chapter Five

The ride home for Samuel was incredible, the velocity at which Dr. Walker drove exhilarating. More importantly, the professor's expression was one of unabashed freedom. Darlene rocked the curves and bends of the road as they traveled the incline into Iroquois Pack territory. Given time, Samuel could write a song about it. The words were already forming in his mind.

"So, you said Dr. Marshall told you about me on purpose?" Samuel asked as they pulled onto the compound. "I don't live in the main house. Turn right beside the rosebushes."

"Ah, your own place? Good. I have to say this property is quite expansive. It's the size of a village."

Fuck, I have never looked forward to getting to my house as I do right now. Patience. I must practice patience. "Yes, it was the request I made when I turned eighteen. If I had to stay on pack grounds, I wanted my own home."

"Pack grounds." Dr. Walker nodded as he drove on, following Samuel's instructions. "Living together as a unit can be wearing, I assume. It's always been just my mothers and me. A few friends here or there, now only Dr. Marshall."

There it was again, Dr. Walker's acceptance for something that would have been weird to anyone else. And along with that, the loneliness in those last few words filled Samuel's heart with sadness for the man.

"There, that's it." It wasn't much, but it was Samuel's. His cottage was his favorite place. He even had a small garden in the back, which paled next to the sprawling grounds his grandfather and Kristoff shared, but he'd only just gotten started. Maybe he had no idea what the plant names were or how much water they required, but they survived and were beautiful. He hadn't even used any magic to encourage them to thrive. He liked to think that proved he was a nurturer.

His front yard was dotted in white flowers and hanging baskets of purple and yellow blooms. The house itself was a lovely lavender with baby-blue-trimmed windows. On his front porch, because he had to have a porch to sit on and read, his favorite spot was a rocking bench that hung next to the door.

The inside consisted of four bedrooms, a small study, and a kitchen he used as much as he was capable—he wasn't a chef. As with the main house, his kitchen was state of the art with all the shiny fixtures, he just wasn't skilled at using them. He enjoyed the rooms he'd converted to a music studio and a library. He especially cherished his en suite bathroom, where he could leisurely soak in his tub. His study where he studied? Okay, watched movies. Hell, Samuel loved every room in his home and the colors he'd splattered all over.

Oh, and the playroom he'd created was his favorite. He'd adorned it with cushions and throws and oh so many toys. He'd enjoyed many good times in that room. So while he wasn't a chef in his fancy kitchen, he did have his talents—tying men up and making them scream being one of them.

"Well, are you going to invite me in?"

Dr. Walker's alluring voice gained his full attention.

Was he? Should he?

Samuel ran his tongue across his teeth. He was nervous, which was a rare feeling for him. This day was a day of firsts, and he wasn't sure he was ready for whatever this first might be.

But he wanted it. More than anything, he craved what Dr. Walker offered.

Part of him was saying no, but no was quickly shifting to a yes.

And then suddenly, the window next to him blew apart, and his world went dark.

Samuel heard shouting . . . loud shouting, and he needed them to stop. He wasn't dead, but he was starting to wish he was. He hurt everywhere. Gentle hands touched his face, his arms, checking and prodding.

"Samuel," a worried voice called to him.

Samuel smiled. He heard other sounds, other voices, but one of the two he needed was repeating his name softly.

"Present and accounted for," Samuel croaked.

"Good, because I've only just met you." Dr. Walker whispered.

A soft kiss on his brow made Samuel almost smile.

"Now, there are people here who are very worried about you, but I refused to let you out of my sight."

Samuel warmed up inside from those words. He liked being cared for . . . had been longing for it for years.

When he opened his eyes, he realized he wasn't in the car or even in his bed. He recognized his childhood bedroom. Kristoff stood next to his bed, eyebrows creased with worry. His grandfather stood next to Kristoff, their hands clasped tightly. His father held his mother, who bounced his youngest sibling, Calypso, on her hip. She appeared angry, her eyes fierce and her face battle-ready.

"It's good to see you awake, my love." She flashed a half-smile. "Now, we need to find out what happened so we can kill whoever tried to take my child from me."

His mother's wings were spread, the tips dagger-sharp. While his father was the warrior, his mother was a force to be reckoned with in her own right. Each of her children was talented, and every one of them knew how to fight. She had insisted that all her babes would be prepared not only mentally but physically, and they were. Well, everyone except Samuel. He'd tried. Okay, not that much. Once lessons were done, he was, too.

As for his siblings, they focused and took to heart that ready-for-battle mantra his father had going. Samuel, not so much. It was a constant frustration for his mother, but he'd never seen the point of it. He had always been safe.

Well, maybe until today.

"Shelly, my lass, I know not that this is what needs to be done. I will secure this threat, but we need to find out what the reason is. Part of that would be answered by this *being* with our bairn, I wager." His father needed hills, a horse, and a war.

That was where Samuel pictured his father whenever he spoke. He almost laughed, but it would hurt too much.

Dr. Walker nodded. "I can't tell you much. I was trying to convince Samuel to let me in." He nodded toward Samuel. "I believe I was almost there when Darlene's window exploded."

"Darlene?" Shelly asked. Her eyes sparked, and thunder rolled. "There wasn't a woman there when we recovered my son."

"It's his car, Mom," Samuel answered, then groaned as he sat up among the bevy of pillows cushioned around him.

"His car?" Kristoff questioned.

Of course, he would be here to see me look foolish.

"Yes, my car's name is Darlene. After her window was destroyed, I tried as best I could to protect Samuel. The shards of glass and the intensity of the blast threw his entire body forward into my arms. I dragged him out quickly."

His mother nodded, handing Calypso over to his father, who lost a little of his fierceness when his young one was in his arms. Calypso rested her head on their father's shoulder and twirled his long red hair around her fingers, gripping it as she nodded off quickly.

His mother stepped forward, scrutinizing Dr. Walker. "You're different than what usually follows him home. You smell different, too. Magic."

"I don't have a real answer for you . . ."

"Shelly. My name is Shelly Tolliver, and I'm a sprite. These men here are wolves, and that boy is a combination of both. Now, what are you?" She peered at Dr. Walker as if she could see beneath the surface of his flesh.

"Again, I don't have an answer that will satisfy your curiosity. I don't honestly know what I am. I know what I can do, what I've seen, but I don't truly know me. Neither do my mothers. I'm more concerned with what happened to my car and why someone tried to harm your son. Shouldn't you be the same?" Dr. Walker's words were infused with calm.

The soothing tone wrapped itself around Samuel and gave him comfort.

"Perhaps knowing what you are would help that," was his mother's icy response. Shelly Tolliver was very protective of her brood, and unknowns were not welcome, especially if that unknown caused one of her babes to be in pain.

"Before you square off, can I have something to drink?" Samuel affected a throaty cough certain to distract his mother from her stare down.

"Oh, Sammy. Yes, of course." She threw a look at Dr. Walker but left the room, presumably to get Samuel something to drink.

"Now, while the lass is gone, I don't give a fuck who you are," his grandfather spoke up. "You're with my grandson. I want to know what has happened so we can protect him. Troublesome brat that he is, he's still mine. I'll have no one thinking they can harm what I was given to shield."

Jeremiah Tolliver was the alpha of the Iroquois Pack for a

reason. His will was ironclad, and he had his second—now alpha mate—to back him in the form of one deadly Kristoff Dumanovsky-Tolliver. Their union had filled an emptiness that existed in the leadership of their pack, and it was one Samuel envied for himself. He wanted what they had. He wanted more than they had. Perhaps now would be his chance to claim his mates. *My Double Ds.*

"I respect your need to know . . . Mr. Tolliver?" Dr. Walker asked to clarify. "But I know nothing more than what I've said. Your grandson's safety was my complete concern, not whoever had damaged my car. I can tell from the people standing here Samuel's well-being is of high import. I have just met him, and I already wish to protect the wayward boy."

"I'm not a boy. I'm an adult." Even to his ears, his words sounded petulant.

"Ah, then, my sweet, you should endeavor to act like one."

Samuel welcomed the tender kiss on his lips. Perhaps he wasn't the only one ready to claim.

"Does Darren know this man, Samuel?" Jeremiah asked.

Instead of giving Samuel time to respond, Dr. Walker answered the question for him. "No, we've only just met, but just like Samuel, I intend to know him well."

Chapter Six

A chill ran through Darren's body. Something was wrong. He thought of the conversation he'd had with Dr. Walker, the man who made him ache for things he'd thought he'd buried. But no, that wasn't what had him standing with ice in his veins in the office with the oldest Milburn. He did his best to pay attention, because being caught ill-prepared by Milburn was a sure way to end the career he was trying to begin.

Still, that feeling couldn't be ignored, but he managed to complete his meeting.

During his drive back to the hotel, the feeling worsened.

It had to be Samuel. And as if to confirm his fear, his phone rang.

"Hello. Samuel? Baby, is everything okay?" Darren answered as his apprehension worsened.

He'd worked hard to finish his tasks and was able to return home early if needed. He'd done the research, spoken to the witnesses, and possibly secured people for the case. So it looked like he could check out now and return to Louisville to see what the hell was happening with Samuel and Dr. Walker.

"Darren, I know I said I would wait, that I would be good, but I need you," Samuel whispered.

Whispering? My Samuel was fearless, not fearful.

"What's wrong, sweetheart? What is it?"

"You know I hate when you call me that."

"Yeah, I know." It was hard keeping himself distant. He

tried not to use endearments. Unfortunately, they just escaped. Especially now. It couldn't be helped. Right now, none of that mattered. "What's wrong, Samuel? I have this feeling."

"Funny you say that." Nervous laughter. "Something happened, and I promise I'm not trying to be a whiny brat right now."

Acknowledgment of his behavior? Darren's heart kicked into overdrive. "You're worrying me, babe. What's going on?"

"I think someone tried to kill me. Dr. Walker was taking me home. When we got here, his car window blew out, glass fucking everywhere. The brigade is here breathing down my back." Samuel spoke through gritted teeth. Frustration and Samuel were not a good combination.

Darren heard words in the background and possible growling.

Dr. Walker and Samuel?

"Fine. Okay, they were worried and felt they should all be here to ask me questions rather than find out where the shots came from. I mean, isn't that what people do? Investigate?" Samuel's snark did little to hide the fear.

"It's okay, Samuel. It will be okay. Give me an hour and a half. I'm on my way." He had to ask. "Is Dr. Walker there?"

"Yes, he's here."

Darren nodded, and even without knowing the man, his anxiety decreased significantly. "Good. Let me talk to him."

There was movement in the background, then that voice that made Darren's dick take notice earlier was on the phone.

"Darren?"

"You have him."

"Yes, I'm not leaving until you get here."

"Okay, thank you. He loves his family. They love him, but . . ."

Darren didn't have to finish.

"I understand." Dr. Walker said. "I have Samuel. We'll get him to eat, and I'll take care of him."

Darren sighed in relief. Dr. Walker was still new to him, but for some reason, he trusted him, had faith in his words and his desire to keep Samuel safe. "It will take me a couple of hours. Tennessee isn't that far."

"I understand, Darren. I assure you I'll be here until you get here, and maybe even after that." Dr. Walker's voice was soothing, a balm to an anxious soul. "Deep breaths, beautiful. I've got him. I've got you, too."

Darren nodded, and while he knew the man keeping his boy safe couldn't see him, it was all he could manage.

After he made the necessary calls, he was on his way.

Hours later, Darren pulled into Samuel's driveway. He loved his guy's place. The purple house with the blue-trimmed windows because Samuel wanted it that way. The plants Samuel collected—like others collected shiny trinkets—decorated the porch beside the wooden rocking bench. Blooms exploded over the small patch of land, along with all the other signs that someone who loved life lived there.

His Samuel.

The dark windows indicated that Samuel wasn't home, which meant he was probably at the alpha's house. Darren's anxiety still rode him hard, but he refused to consider the what-ifs of the situation. He needed to know what was going on.

Darren pulled out of the driveway and hit the accelerator, speeding until he'd arrived at the main house. He hopped out of the car, allowing himself a brief moment to stretch since he hadn't stopped once on the way. His ride was comfortable, though. It should be. He'd paid enough for it after Samuel threatened to buy something more expensive if he didn't do it himself.

Darren had no doubt Samuel would have kept his promise. So he'd bought a car that wouldn't hurt him financially but would keep his little wolf off his back.

There were no locked doors on pack lands, something Darren considered worrisome now. There was being confident, and there was being obtuse. Not securing doors because it was assumed no one would cross pack borders was foolish. Yes, creatures who walked the property could give lesser men nightmares, but that didn't stop some from pushing limits.

Still, Darren was grateful when he could enter without any obstacles. He strode through the living room and back to Samuel's old room, past the library where one of the little ones appeared to be sleeping on a chair and right on to where he could hear people talking.

"I'm not moving back to the compound. I have my own home. I like it there," Samuel argued.

The rage building in Samuel's voice worried Darren more than anything else.

"Samuel," a calming voice soothed.

Darren recognized the timbre of the voice he'd heard over the phone earlier. When he entered the room, there were objects gently levitating in the air, items circling. He pulled a few from the air and set them down before making his way to Samuel's bedside.

He kept his gaze on Samuel only and not the lean, beautiful man lying next to him, then knelt beside the bed and opened his arms. Suddenly he had a warm, shaking Samuel squeezing him close, breathing him in deeply.

"Darren, son. Glad to have you home. Perhaps you can talk some sense into him." Jeremiah growled, an audible struggle to contain the patience he often wielded as alpha.

"His room has been maintained. Everything here for his comfort." Conner certainly wasn't helping matters.

Samuel was one of Connor's many young but no longer a child. He was a grown man. Although there were times when he challenged even Darren's patience.

"He has a home," Darren said. "I'm sorry, but if he doesn't want to stay with you, it can't be forced."

"It is not safe," Jeremiah insisted. Jeremiah was a good alpha who loved every member of his pack, but Samuel didn't see himself as pack. The foreign blood running through his veins made him question obedience, which was why his home was his sanctuary, one that would take a crowbar for him to be removed from. Even now, Darren could tell Samuel was chafing here, ready to go home.

Samuel had worked hard to earn his plot of ground, his patch of independence. Darren would help him keep it. It wasn't that Darren failed to understand the need to keep him safe from his future. He just had no idea why Samuel's family didn't get that their love was suffocating.

He'd never had that. His grandmother had his back, had loved him, fought for him, and taught him to fight for himself. She'd never confined him. She taught him how to fly and was the buttress for his wings. Samuel needed some of that, a gentle push but with a tug to let him know that he was safe, tethered.

That was what Darren worked to give him. He wanted to give him more. So much more. He just didn't know if he could.

But in this, Darren would not fail him. He wouldn't hesitate to show he had his back, that it was all right to fight for himself. "I understand, Alpha. And Samuel understands." Darren ignored the distinct growl from Samuel's wolf. "He may not want to, but he does. But you trying to force him to live in this house is not what he needs."

House, ha. As if one could call the sprawling home shared by inner circle of the pack a *house.* It boasted enough rooms for twenty people to live comfortably, three floors and two balconies that stretched out over a lush garden. Sariah's garden, Jeremiah's first mate. It was the pride of the pack, the grounds extensive and meticulously cared for by pack experts. Magazines now featured the blooms of their roses and the orchids they were now known to cultivate there. With Kristoff's return to the pack, visits to the pack gardens were re-established, and field trips for schools in the area resumed. The pack was thriving.

It was home, not just for the pack but for Darren as well. His grandmother was buried on pack grounds. And though he had his apartment now, it was here he spent the holidays and here where he celebrated occasions with a people that allowed him to be a part of their inner sanctum.

And it was here that he met the man who would always have his heart.

"We don't even know if this was about him. Perhaps it was an accident. Someone hunting a little too close to pack grounds," Darren speculated.

Conner nodded, his large fingers dragging through his thick red beard. "We considered that, but my men checked around his little house, and my son had visitors of the sneaky kind. There are signs of window tampering, sticks broken. It bears watching."

"So what?" Samuel grumbled.

Darren sighed and turned to his stubborn friend. Opening his arms, he laughed when Samuel climbed him with legs wrapping easily around his waist. Darren knew how scent-sensitive the beings here were and hoped they didn't smell how that little act of Samuel's made him horny as hell.

He held Samuel close and sighed when Samuel scent-marked him, his wild hair tickling his cheek.

A throat cleared, and Darren hummed when a wide hand covered his shoulder.

"I have an idea," Dr. Walker said.

"The creature speaks," Jeremiah growled, then took a breath. "What are you, Professor Walker? You are more than human. I recognize something in you, something familiar."

"I have no ready answer for you, Alpha Jeremiah. I know very little of my origin. I know I am more than human. My mothers have for years, as they are the ones who accepted a strange foundling into their home. Taught him to pretend to be human and later to accept that he never would be."

Jeremiah looked doubtful, but there was interest in his jeweled blue eyes that couldn't be ignored. "Foundling. How old?"

"I arrived at my mothers' home at the age of twelve, spoke very little, but I could cause terror. I walked in other's dreams, something I later learned to pull back." The story was one the professor had shared before, it seemed.

Darren's throat nearly closed. It couldn't be, not when he'd done all he could never to cross the path of one.

"Dreams, you say?" Kristoff focused on Darren, the warning of silence unnecessary.

Darren was frozen in place, his arms wrapped around Samuel tightly as he held himself together.

"Yes, I can follow a person's thoughts as they sleep or even when they are awake. They need only drift for me to slip in. It is a talent I've had for years. One that I've shared with very few."

Darren felt the professor's body against his hard, solid, and somehow protective.

"I find myself drawn to these two. A connection." There was a darkness in the professor's words. "First, I thought it was Samuel. It was, but not alone. He was the thread to Darren. And now, with both of them here, I find I may finally have my home. I won't let anything happen to either of them." His hand slid down Darren's back and rested at the curve of his ass.

The professor's words danced along Darren's skin, taking his breath away. It was too soon to trust those words, to believe the truth he heard there. But he did. He believed.

"If you think you're going to take my son and his . . ." Conner started, then paused.

What was he going to say?

"Yes," Samuel said. "Yes, I'm going with the professor. We both are." His words were steel, his resolve unwavering. "Right, Darren?"

Darren wanted to refuse, but he said the only thing he could. "Yes."

There was something about these two men. The beautiful fiery creature Dailon couldn't wait to possess. And the protector that made him crave things he told himself he could never have.

Dailon had no idea what made him hunt down the boy after Ali had described him, but Dailon had known deep within his soul he needed this person. Samuel had fascinated the jaded man who'd accepted Dailon as a friend long ago. Ali had looked beyond Dailon's walls and leaped over them until Dailon had finally acknowledged their friendship. He valued Ali's opinion, so there was no question about him discovering why Samuel.

Ali had liked the boy, had bragged about his sharp retorts and astute observations. Dailon couldn't resist seeing the creature for himself. And when he'd seen him? Wild fiery hair blended with red, blonde, and honey golden strands, a lithe frame begging to be caressed. Flame and smoke. Dailon had inhaled it from afar. Combustible. The mind, a spark he wanted to taste.

Dailon hungered to explore Samuel's dreams, to run through his mind and take him, own him, and worship him. But the boy's mind was resistant to his touch, something keeping Samuel closed off from him.

There was a key to Samuel's mind, and there was no way Dailon could gain entrance without it. He'd found the key when he'd first heard Samuel on the phone with his friend.

Darren.

Darren was the key. Not only to the luscious garden of Samuel's mind, but also the key to Dailon's inner spirit.

The alpha wolf had asked what he was. It was a question he'd had no idea how to answer. Dailon wasn't a wolf. He wasn't a witch like his mothers. He wasn't whatever Samuel's mother was. Neither was he human.

But in that room, he sensed the alpha knew a secret, one he would not share. A secret that involved Darren, Dailon was certain of it.

It had nearly taken a battle to get his family to allow him to leave with them. In the end, Samuel proved his mettle and refused to be cowed by his overprotective clan. He'd packed the things his family had brought to his childhood home, glaring them down as he did so. He'd grabbed his duffel and satchel, kissed his mother on her cheek, and walked out of his bedroom. Darren's lopsided smile had warmed Dailon's dark soul as he followed Samuel out of the house, leaving Dailon to close the door on Samuel's family in their home.

They'd decided to ride together in Darren's beast of a car. Darren was a big man, dressed in a bespoke suit and possessed a charisma Dailon wanted to lick from head to toe. His car was a large black SUV with tinted windows, making Samuel look even smaller in the back seat, his eyes shadowed with exhaustion. On the way to Dailon's house, Samuel crashed, his eyes fluttering closed as if fighting to stay awake.

It was sweet the way Darren had looked back at Samuel, his eyes filled with so much want, desire, and yet a tenderness he'd tried to hide earlier.

"Why don't you tell him," Dailon asked as he turned on Bardstown Road and then took the road to the left, putting them on the path to his home.

"I think he already knows," Darren murmured.

Dailon admired that, the honesty there. "It's obvious to me with the way he curved into you, he loves you. You love him. A blind man could see it."

I see it. I want it.

"I do, but proving to him I'm worth it is the problem," was Samuel's groggy input from the back.

"Samuel," Darren groaned.

"Save it, Darren. I'm too tired, and my nerves are too shot to argue with you. Us not being together? Stupid. Dailon sees it. I see it. The only one who won't accept it is you."

Dailon almost shivered from hearing his name on Samuel's lips. It made him thirst, made him want to nibble at Samuel's plump lips and take him right there against the car, show Darren how that sweet form could be used. He needed to hear Samuel beg. He wanted to listen to both men plead for release.

But he had to wait. It wasn't time. Too much had happened, so Dailon would be patient for at least tonight. Tomorrow was a new day, one filled with promise.

Inside his home, he couldn't resist and drew Darren to him, slid his arm around his wide shoulders, and brought him close.

"You know he's right," Dailon murmured. "Cease this floundering resistance and give him want he wants. You."

Darren looked at him with hope in his eyes, and Dailon would have been a fool not to obey his own words.

He bent his head and took those lips that deserved to be kissed. Life and energy, sparkling and potent. This was what Dailon craved. He sank into the taste of the man, breathed him in as he savored the pleasure there.

"Well," Samuel said. "That should piss me off. This close to what I've always wanted for myself, and here you are enjoying him. You don't know him. You barely even know me. Why the fuck are we so eager to be kissed by you? Touched by you?" Samuel sighed.

And while he longed to dive into Samuel's breath, he was focused on drinking in the taste of Darren.

Darren felt good in Dailon's arms, his body leaning into him. He drew Darren closer, enjoying the sighs and moans.

When they came up for air, Darren looked up, his dark brown eyes dazed as if he'd been drugged. He nibbled at his lips and stepped back, looking at Samuel as if asking for forgiveness, then back to Dailon in confusion.

"I think I need to go to bed, alone. I need to go to bed alone." Darren's voice shook.

Dailon would have felt sorry for him if he had it in him, but he lacked the guilt. He'd lived so long on the border of darkness that he'd learned to embrace it. Instead, he wanted to push Darren further, see if he could make him break, and lose that rigid control he held. He smiled but knew his smile wasn't friendly or even kind. He knew what he looked like when he gave in to his need.

He stepped into Darren's space, not allowing him room to run. "And what if I said no, Darren?" He dragged Darren back to him, bent his head for another kiss. "You smell so good. The way you feel, the way you taste. I thirst for you. I told myself I would give you time, but it was a lie. Tonight, I will have you, listen to your screams. I will fuck you deep and slow, then watch you fuck Samuel. Tonight." He shoved Darren and enjoyed his look of surprise at being slammed against a wall.

Darren wasn't a small man. At around 6'4 and built like a wide receiver, he was all muscle. Dailon's frame was more swimmer, and most people had no idea how strong he was until he showed them.

Part of it was the darkness. The rest of it was all him.

"Samuel, I want to see Darren's skin. All of it. Be a good boy and help him out of his clothes."

Samuel took in a sharp breath. "Darren?"

"I didn't ask, Samuel. Do as I say."

Darren turned to Samuel, following his movements fearfully. He didn't speak, didn't protest, as Samuel lost the weariness that had enveloped him when they arrived.

Samuel smiled, and Dailon would almost swear that grin was darker than his own. Darren stood stock still as Samuel went to him. Samuel turned back to Dailon, and he nodded his approval.

They stood in the foyer of his home, the chandelier catching the moonlight from the open roof. A blue glow danced over their skin from the tint of the window, greatly accenting the tableau before him.

Dailon waited, his hands itching to shred Darren's clothes himself, but the desire to see Samuel have what he'd ached for so long was stronger.

"Samuel," Darren pleaded.

"No, Darren. Not anymore. I want this, want you. I won't lose this moment. I won't have it taken away from me."

Dailon admired the strength he heard there. Samuel deserved this, and tonight Dailon would ensure he received it.

"Please," Darren murmured.

This time Dailon didn't know if that meant *please stop* or *please go on*. He unbuttoned his cuffs and loosened his tie.

"I was wondering on the way here how Samuel's lips would look stretched around your dick. I wonder if he can take two? I'd like to feel my dick next to yours covered in his spit," Dailon said. He walked down the hallway, picking up a chair and laughing when he returned to see that no one had moved.

While Samuel was determined, he still required direction. That was why Dailon was there.

My specialty.

"Samuel, my sweet, thank you for waiting for me. Let me arrange myself for a perfect view." Dailon set his chair down, crossed his legs, and prepared to enjoy the show. Sighing, he said, "I want to see his nipples."

Dailon enjoyed Darren's quiet gasp of anticipation. It appeared a little encouragement was all Samuel needed, because he leaned into Darren's space quickly, breathing him in deeply.

"You want me?" Samuel asked. The way he moved against Darren could be likened to an animal sniffing its prey.

"Wanting you was never a question, Samuel. Having you was. Keeping you was. Wanting you? I've suffered from the want of having you next to me for years now." Darren's voice was a harsh whisper.

The sound thrummed along Dailon's nerve endings.

"Then why?" Samuel asked as he placed his hands beneath Darren's shirt sliding his fingers along Darren's skin.

Darren hissed, and the sound made Dailon's dick rock hard, pressing against the zipper of his slacks.

"Your claws, Samuel." Darren moaned, and his voice was rough with the obvious need written over every muscle of his body.

"I can't help it, Darren. I've been forced to control myself around you for years. To touch you like this, my hands on your warm skin? My beast is too near the surface to be denied. The way I feel, I ache so much, I hurt with the need for more of you."

Dailon heard Darren's cotton shirt tear and hummed when he saw Darren's exposed chest.

"Shit." Darren groaned when Samuel's head bent. He shivered and trapped his arms against the wall behind him as if trying to hold himself back.

Ah. Darren is fighting to restrain himself. There will be none of that.

CHAPTER SEVEN

Darren knew he needed to stop this, but he couldn't. He wouldn't touch Samuel, but he hungered for Samuel's touches, aching for the skin against skin contact. It wasn't right. His life was destined for another, some unknown he refused to accept. He didn't want to fail Samuel. Someday, a creature would come for him, a Sandman like Aiden or like that asshole Keith, a monster who still hunted Darren's nightmares. Whatever he started with Samuel would be for nothing—a broken dream. Because he and that being would be drawn to each other, his life only there to support something he hoped never to see.

But he couldn't think of that now, not when Samuel's heat was this close, his honey golden eyes glowing with his beast.

Still, Darren didn't touch. Perhaps if he kept his clasping fingers against this wall, if he remembered not to wrap his arms around Samuel's smaller frame, he could control himself. He hadn't counted on the professor, though. Walker.

While Samuel shredded his shirt, Walker stood and walked toward them. Darren swallowed, the determined look on Walker's face scaring the hell out of him.

Walker stood next to him and grasped one of his hands with long tapered fingers. They could be the hands of an artist, smooth. But they were strong, too, as Walker placed Darren's hand onto Samuel's shoulder.

"Touch him, Darren. You want this. You are wasting this moment on foolish resistance when you could have the very treasure you've longed for all this time," Walker murmured.

The professor was a tricky bastard. One who seemed to know more than any person should about what Darren desired. It was like the man could read his mind.

Yes, Darren wanted. He wanted to taste the stars and moons that raced over Samuel's skin and down his collarbone. He wanted to lick across Samuel's too warm skin and sink his teeth in.

He wanted more.

And before he realized it, he bent to lick designs he'd watched inked onto Samuel's skin. He'd been there the day Samuel had gotten them, his salutation to the energy that called to him. The tattoo artist had wondered about the sudden darkening of clouds and the wind that appeared outside, but Darren hadn't worried. He'd acknowledged Samuel's power and welcomed it while Samuel had the signs of his power marked on his body. The blue wisps of wind that weaved over his shoulder and the leaves that spun across his back were revealed as Darren pulled Samuel's shirt off his body.

"So beautiful," he whispered with reverence. His. *Samuel is mine.* He was too overcome with pleasure to deny the truth now. It didn't help that the devil on his shoulder actually stood next to him, urging him to take and keep, to savor and possess.

"Yes, so beautiful," Walker agreed as he moved to stand behind Samuel.

Darren shivered as he watched Walker's eyes shift. Sharp blue irises changed, becoming mercury and then bottomless blues and grays with silvery streaks dancing within. He was lost in their depths until Samuel nipped at him, then he was lost to Samuel once again.

Samuel's body shivered before he moaned with pleasure. "More," he begged.

"Of course, Samuel," Walker said, his words raspy with

need. "I have you, little one. We have you. Focus on you. Take whatever you need."

Samuel's head rose, and his eyes glowed brightly with the power he could no longer contain. "Darren," he growled.

Darren was helpless.

There would be no more resisting.

He was Samuel's.

Samuel fell back into Walker's arms, dragging Darren with him, kissing him roughly. Darren gasped at the copper taste of blood on Darren's tongue.

Darren looked up to see Walker watching him, his expression hungry and wanting. Darren had done that. He and Samuel had cracked Walker's control.

He smiled, then, feeling daring, asked him, "See something you want, Walker?"

Walker returned the smile. "Yes, I want to have you, both of you, in my bed right now. Bring him, Samuel."

Samuel didn't waste any time. He gripped Darren's wrist tightly and followed Walker's tight ass through the foyer, down the hall, and turning to the left to walk into a bedroom. One of the room's walls was made of glass from top to bottom, open to the forest beyond. Whatever they did would be exposed for the world to see.

Darren couldn't give a damn. *I am so ready to fuck and get fucked.*

He almost laughed when Samuel threw him on the bed, then made quick work of his clothes. The ratty t-shirt he wore and his favorite threadbare gray sweats were yanked off, leaving Samuel completely nude before him.

Samuel had always been beautiful to him. Standing there, he was glorious, his pale skin glowing in the moonlight, his long cock standing out between his legs, big and thick and primed for Darren's hole.

Walker stood next to him with way too many clothes on.

Darren couldn't resist the temptation to taunt him. "Well, Walker? You going to do something about that boa constrictor behind your zipper?"

Walker shook his head slowly. "You're asking for my hand on your sweet ass, Darren."

"Promises, promises," Darren teased, emboldened by the look Samuel was giving him.

Samuel continued to stare as he stroked his dick from balls to head, sliding his thumb over the tip in the glistening precum Darren could see there. Darren licked his lips, wanting to taste.

"Finish what you started, Samuel," Walker said as his eyes roved over Darren's body.

"Yes, Dailon," Samuel sang with a feral glint sparkling in his eyes.

And it was a song that played on Darren's heartstrings.

Samuel strode toward him and knelt on the bed, his cock bouncing as he moved. He grabbed Darren's jeans and popped open the button, then tugged them over Darren's hips and down his legs. In seconds he was back, looking down at Darren, hope filling his eyes.

"I don't know, Samuel," Darren muttered. "I just . . . I want this moment. I want you. I just—"

His mouth was suddenly filled with the taste of Samuel, the sweetness too delicious to continue with excuses. Root beer from their drive because Samuel had to have his favorite soda after they left his house. Cinnamon, too. If Samuel was going to have his favorite soda, he might as well have his favorite candy.

When Samuel ended the kiss, he whispered, "Shut up, Darren. We're going to enjoy this. You and me and the professor, who is sliding his hands along the crack of my ass. I'm not asking you for anything else right now."

But the way Samuel's eyes softened when they looked at

him said he was giving him an out, offering him forgiveness. Darren wanted to make promises, present Samuel with forever, but he couldn't. Not right now. Probably not ever.

Instead, he reached up and pulled Samuel back down, tasting more of him, begging for anything Samuel was willing to give. Samuel moaned into his throat, growling, making it obvious his beast was rising again.

It wasn't often Samuel allowed the beings within free rein, and for him to show an inkling of them now spoke to just how out of control he was feeling. The wolf Darren knew for certain existed. The sprite, too. But there were times when he believed there were more.

The bed dipped slightly, and Darren opened his eyes to see Walker with his arms wrapped around Samuel's waist, reaching around to squeeze Samuel's ample cock.

"You have on too many clothes," Darren said.

Walker laughed. "Such a flirt when you're freed from the restraints of your mind, Darren. Don't worry about me. Tonight is just about you and Samuel. Making sure you both have what you need. Each other. Tomorrow is a different day."

Walker eased back and pushed Samuel's ass cheeks apart, then his head disappeared. Darren couldn't see what he was doing but imagined the wetness of his tongue driving into Samuel's ass.

"Fuck, Dailon," Samuel groaned. "Any of your students know how well you can eat ass? Shit."

Darren loved Samuel's filthy mouth just as much as Walker seemed to love Samuel's ass. Samuel moaned, and Darren reached between them to stroke Samuel's cock.

"More. So good, Darren. Deeper, Dailon. My Double Ds. Oh, yeah. Fuck. Darren, want your mouth on my dick right fucking now."

Darren hurried to do his bidding, shifting from beneath

Samuel, who dropped to all fours on the bed with Walker still sucking and licking at his ass. Darren turned and prostrated himself, positioning his body in a way that would give him access to that long dick he'd wanted to taste for years. He didn't hesitate, simply took down the entire length of it until it lodged in the back of his throat. He moaned, his mouth so full with Samuel he could barely breathe.

"Yes," Samuel growled and shoved, fucking Darren's throat while Walker munched on his ass.

Darren groaned, allowing Samuel to shove his dick in further. He held onto Samuel's slim thighs for balance as Samuel used him.

Samuel growled again. "So good. Both of you make me feel so fucking good. More tongue."

Samuel cried out after Darren heard what must have been Walker smacking his ass.

"Manners, Samuel," Walker growled. "Say please. "

"Why?"

Samuel cried out again, the slap on his ass loud in the room. Darren relished the flavor when Samuel's cock spurted precum.

There was nothing in the stars that could have predicted this moment for Samuel today. Here he was, his ass receiving an extraordinary reaming, the voracious licking and sucking the professor was doing enough to make him beg.

Samuel never begged. Never pleaded.

But then, he'd never had the person he wanted more than life on offer before him. He'd never had the lips he'd watched laugh and talk late into the night wrapped around his cock, creating the most phenomenal suction he'd ever had.

Samuel could write songs about those lips, sing them at his band's venues. He would scream loud about the tenderness of Darren's tongue against his balls. He would create lyrics about Darren's brown eyes and how they caught the subtle rays of light in the room as he looked up at Samuel when he rose after Dailon's slap on his ass.

Dailon wanted him to say please. Wasn't that begging? Why should he, when all he'd ever had to do was nudge, encourage? Normally, he could create the circumstance he needed to take what he wanted, but not here. This moment was not of his making. Earlier, he'd been shot at through a car window, and were the person a better marksman, he could have been injured. Now, Samuel was having his ass eaten and his dick sucked, and he wanted more. He could have missed this, never had it.

"Samuel," Dailon warned, his hand palming the curve of Samuel's ass.

It smarted. There'd be a welt there.

Does Dailon like that? Making my ass red?

The way Dailon's voice deepened to a near growl certainly sounded like it.

"Please suck my dick harder and give me more of your fucking tongue, Darren," Samuel ground out.

Dailon's laugh was rich, and Samuel loved it. The timbre of the man's voice made the sucking Darren was doing all that much better.

Darren moaned beneath him and gave him more of his tongue, curving it around his balls, lapping at both.

"Oh, yeah. That's good, Darren. So good." Samuel's breath hitched when Dailon added fingers to his hole, his reward, he supposed, for saying please. It was a stretch and burn Samuel could appreciate after Dailon's wet attentions. He welcomed the bite of pain. Coupled with Darren's suction, he writhed with wild pleasure, but it still wasn't enough. Almost there but not at the crest, he was a pendulum of unreleased desires. When Dailon pressed a finger against his magical button, he nearly exploded.

"There you go, sweetheart. Feels good, yes. You have no idea how much I would love to fuck you right now, your hole filled with my swollen cock. I can wait, though." Dailon punctuated his last words with another direct hit, making Samuel cry out. "I love the sounds you make. But what I would like to see most? Right now? Your dick inside Darren's sweet round ass. Have you imagined it? I know you have. Look at him bowing, worshipping at the altar of your pretty piece of meat. It's been hard not to cum myself from listening to his sounds." Dailon struck again, and Samuel bit his lip with need.

At the mention of his name, Darren looked up. Samuel was surprised to see the interest reflected in Darren's eyes. The wonder.

Had this been Dailon's plan all along? For Samuel to be inside of Darren?

"Darren, let's give Samuel what he really wants. What I know you want. That's what will do it for me tonight. You on your knees, your ass owned by our Samuel."

Our. That three-letter word made Samuel spurt again. He wanted that, wanted to belong to someone. He wanted someone to feel he was worth claiming, worth keeping. It was his secret, the need to be kept and treasured.

With his family, he had to prove he was strong enough, independent enough, and show the damage he could do so they would stop trying to coddle him. His father was Conner Tolliver, one of the most dangerous wolves in his grandfather's pack. When Samuel had shown little interest in ripping heads off and hunting down the enemy, they had assumed he needed to be protected instead.

Then there was his fun with nature. The sprite in him gloried in a challenge and enjoyed playing with the elements to see what would happen. He lacked boundaries, knowing when enough was enough. He wanted more. He was a creature of fancy who flew with the wind.

Ethereal.

But he wanted that balance and wanted to be kept. He needed someone to ground him. Maybe one wasn't enough.

Maybe he needed two.

He growled and looked down to see Darren watching him, his tongue sliding over the flared head of his dick.

"I'm going to fuck you, Darren." He didn't miss the warmth in Darren's eyes, the need. *Have I overlooked it before?*

Samuel hadn't realized what his best friend had desired, so happy to just have him in his life. He was the one person Samuel had been careful with, his treasure.

Darren crawled onto the bed, lying back and waiting.

"On your knees, Darren," Dailon commanded, still thrusting his fingers in Samuel's ass. Then he bent and whispered, "Praise him, Samuel. He wants this. He's been waiting to please you. He just needs a push. Push him. Fuck him. Make him yours. One day, you and I will make him bleed. Tonight, help him trust that you will take care of him."

Samuel shivered. The thought of Darren's blood twisted something inside of him. He wanted to taste it. He longed for it, but he could wait. Trust. That was what Darren needed now before Samuel could claim him. Knowing he would wait didn't stop his gums from aching as his teeth swiftly shifted form, the canines sharper. He ran his tongue across one, slicing it. The burn made his dick hard.

"There you are, Samuel. A feast."

And Darren was, his beautifully curved ass in the air, thighs wide so both Samuel and Dailon could get a look at his hole. This time it was Samuel who would do the feasting. He bent and swiped at Darren's hole with his tongue, rejoicing when Darren full-body shivered and shoved his ass back for more.

Dailon's hands worked Samuel with a set of fingers in his

ass, another set squeezing his balls and tugging his cock. Samuel angled to give Dailon more access as he spread Darren's cheeks, diving in. He used his tongue to spear Darren's hole, opening him up before sliding two fingers in, ready to hurry this thing along so he could get inside and have Darren's heat wrapped around his cock.

"Shit, Samuel. Baby."

Samuel stilled. It was the first time Darren had said his name that way. Sure, he'd used the endearment before, but he'd never moaned out the word in desperation. He smiled and forced another finger in.

"Oh, fuck. Samuel, please. Please, baby. Please." Darren's pleas as he shoved his ass back for more was too much to resist.

And Samuel was beyond resisting.

"Patience, Darren," Dailon said. "You've waited so long for this. You can wait a bit more while I slide this lubed condom onto Samuel. After this, we'll all produce those bits of paper so we won't require them. Won't we?" To punctuate his words, he slapped Samuel's ass.

He yelped in surprise. "Yes, fuck. My ass hurts, Dailon."

"I can see my handprint on your ass, Samuel. It's lovely."

The tenderness there made Samuel preen. He'd pleased Dailon, made him happy from just wearing his marks. It was a small thing, but the feeling was huge.

"Darren?" Dailon asked.

"Yes, papers. I have papers. I haven't been with anyone." Darren answered quickly.

Dailon slid his hand along Darren's back until he reached and squeezed his ass. Then he stood and stepped away, and Samuel heard the unmistakable sound of a zipper opening. He imagined Dailon pulling out his dick as he watched them, but he didn't turn to look.

Darren did, though, and the way his eyes widened made

Samuel want to giggle.

"Fucker is huge," Darren said before turning around.

Dailon chuckled. "No worries. I'll make it fit, Darren. I plan to fuck you both at some point. For now, I'm just enjoying the view. That hole of yours is going to need some practice. I don't hold back. I desire to hear you scream."

Samuel moved in behind Darren, ready to give him what they both needed. Dailon's promises were too much, and Samuel was beyond frustrated. His hole was open from Dailon's ministrations but not satisfied. There was one thing he needed to make the ache go away. *I need to fuck Darren right the fuck now.*

He lay on top of Darren, skin to skin, his aching cock against the curve of Darren's ass. "I'm going to fuck you. I've wanted this my whole life. I want to feel your heartbeat on the end of my cock. I want to drink from your neck while I do it. You're not ready, though. I can be patient until you are. But tonight, I'm going to shove my dick so far up your ass you won't be able to overthink this. You'll only be able to beg." It was a promise he intended to keep.

Darren trembled again. "Please, Samuel."

Samuel didn't need any more encouragement. He spread Darren's ass open and shoved his way home, the pre-lubed condom combined with the spit he'd used earlier providing the ease but not reducing the friction he craved. He thrust, fucking Darren, who begged and pleaded for more. Samuel gave him that as he pulled his legs open to give himself more room.

Darren's hole was tight, the perfect fit for Samuel's dick. The way Darren milked him made him want to beg. Before he did precisely that, he angled himself until he was pinging Darren's prostate with every stroke.

"Shit," Darren growled. "Right there, baby." Darren reached back and opened his cheeks to give Samuel more room.

"Lovely," Dailon murmured in the background.

Samuel smiled at the man who'd helped his wishes come true. He could see Dailon in his periphery, but his focus remained on Darren. Fucking him into delirium, eliciting pleas and cries for more. He'd had no idea Darren was this loud, but he loved it.

"Yes, Darren. I love your music, your ass. Squeeze my dick, Darren." Samuel fell against Darren, wrapping his arms around him as much as he could. He loved the strength there and the vulnerability. He licked a line up the middle of Darren's back and smiled when Darren moaned decadently.

"Like that, do you?" Dailon asked. He laughed as he sat on the bed next to them and reclined on the pillow near enough to pet them both, but at a distance where he could still watch. It seemed that was Dailon's favorite thing right then, getting them started and watching the outcome. Samuel would allow that.

Now, he focused on the sweaty man beneath him moaning his name, his brown skin shiny with moisture, muscles stretching as he reached forward grasping.

"Shit," Darren hissed.

Yes, Samuel had nailed just the right spot with that move. He hit it again.

"Fuck."

He bent and kissed Darren on his shoulder. "So beautiful, Darren. I've waited years for this, hoping that you would let me have you."

"Samuel," Darren cried.

"There you go, baby. I have you. You want more. I can give you more. I would give you anything." Samuel thrust again and again, deeper each time.

Yeah, he wanted what Dailon offered. He wanted to come inside Darren, slide his dick between Darren's cheeks, slippery with his seed.

Yeah, there would be papers.

Then he would have the right.

Dailon leaned over and kissed him, and his lips were delicious. He could taste himself there. He grunted into Dailon's mouth as he pumped himself inside Darren.

Dailon pulled away, his eyes slipping into mercury once again. "Turn him over. I want to fuck his pretty face."

Darren was lost in bliss. His ass was filled to splitting with Samuel's cock, and his mouth was crammed with Walker's dick. He was a slut for this.

How did Walker know?

Darren's legs were spread wide, the two men sharing him, taking their pleasure. Samuel's hands gripped his thighs tightly, and there would be bruises and scratches later from the claws he still hadn't sheathed. Darren would probably touch those later, remembering tonight.

Walker held Darren's head between his hands as he shoved his cock into his throat. "Such a sweet mouth. Deep breaths, Darren. There you go. A little more," He crooned as he slid more of his wide head into Darren. "Love the way your lips look stretched so obscenely around my length. Another breath. Getting easier now."

Darren felt wetness slide down his cheeks.

Walker growled. "That's it. Fuck him harder, Samuel. Get ready to swallow, Darren. Your mouth is lovely, so warm. I enjoy the way your throat is stroking my cock. Now, Samuel."

Walker straddled Darren's chest, his pants open far enough for his dick to use Darren's mouth unmercifully. He took a thumb and picked up one of Darren's tears, tasting it, and grinned down as he shoved in further.

Darren loved it. When he felt Samuel tremble and heard his roar of completion, he moaned around Walker's girth, then hummed when the man emptied himself down his throat.

"Yes, Darren. Yes, you are a gift. All of you. More. Lick it. Lick my dick. There you go. Get it all."

Darren sighed, completely fucked out as he followed Walker's commands.

Darren kept licking, cleaning the dick that slid along his lips when Samuel eased out of his ass. He hissed when Samuel wiped at his hole with a damp cloth.

"I'm going to fuck you next, Darren." Walker smiled. "I'm a grower, I'm told."

Shit, if Walker got bigger than the monster that had nearly strangled him, Darren was in for a ride.

He smiled.

Chapter Eight

Darren cracked his eyes open, the light from the windows sliding along his face, piercing his retina wherever he turned. He couldn't move. He was trapped in a tangle of arms and legs.

What the fuck?

Then he remembered, felt the soreness in his jaw and the delicious ache in his ass. He sighed. He was more relaxed and comfortable than he ever had been when he first awoke. No, he was typically fighting for air or trying to run. Escape.

His dreams were often nightmares, but last night had been beautiful, and his sleep peaceful. When the tendrils of his terror had threatened, they were instantly vanquished, and for the first time in forever, he felt rested.

He didn't want to think about Keith, the first Dreamwalker he had ever met. A Sandman, like Aiden, Danny's husband. He'd stopped calling Danny Mr. T years ago when he'd married Aiden. They were friends now, closer to father and son. Though Danny looked young enough to be his brother, he was older by at least twenty years or more, but being the Coimeádaí of a Sandman gave him benefits.

Coimeádaí. That was a destiny Darren didn't want, but Keith had known what he was. It was the reason he'd chosen to take him to threaten Danny. Years had passed, and he could still feel the man's touch. It had followed him into his dreams. But not this past night.

He'd been fucked into oblivion, kissed and caressed. He'd been treated like a treasure, then he'd slept, secure in the arms of Walker and Samuel.

It was good, this feeling.

Safe.

At the moment, the only thing not good was the sun rays tapping his eyeballs.

He sighed and would have stretched but couldn't.

"There you are, my sweet." Walker kissed him on his shoulder. "Welcome to my home."

He could still taste Walker from the night before and wanted to again. It was different. Walker was different. Addicting.

The band around his legs was released, and a curly head of hair slid along his chest until Samuel was facing him, his big brown eyes soft and questioning. Darren smiled at him.

Samuel smiled back. "When can I fuck you again?"

Darren laughed, wild and carefree. Happy. "Samuel."

"No seriously. Can I fuck you now?"

This time it was Walker who responded. "Samuel, let's get some food in the man. Then we all need to talk about what happened last night."

"That's why I'm asking."

Darren tried stretching again and moaned when a wide hand wrapped around his dick, pulling gently.

"Not that, Samuel. We'll need to speak about the bullet that tried to shatter my car window," Walker said while slowly jerking Darren off, sliding his body up until his hard dick notched in the crease of Darren's ass. "Like that, don't you?"

"Mm," was Darren's verbal response while his physical one was rocking his hips back to meet Walker's movements.

When Samuel rose to kiss him, sliding his tongue between Darren's lips, Darren welcomed him. He rocked against Walker's dick, pumped into the man's grip, and savored Samuel's kiss.

His orgasm rolled inside his balls, and he roared when his

dick spurted his seed. He shivered when Samuel moved down to lap at his dick, cleaning him.

Walker growled. "Now, Samuel, you know you should share."

After a shower, which Walker insisted they take separately to give them time to think, they sat outside on the patio. The man was a good cook, evidenced by the bounty of food placed before them.

Darren picked up a piece of bacon and enjoyed the satisfying crunch. The cracked pepper was good, and the bacon was sweet. *Maple?*

He opened his eyes to see the men watching him, Samuel with longing and Walker deep in thought. "Yes?"

Walker smirked. "I don't think I've ever seen anyone make love to bacon before."

"Darren loves to eat, but he works out and plays sports. Being a lawyer keeps him on his toes. It also keeps him away," Samuel said, and no one could miss the bite on the end.

"But I come home, Samuel. I always do," Darren said softly.

Samuel nodded and continued peeling the orange in his hand. "You do."

Darren smiled. "I always will."

Samuel's smile was small, but Darren could still see it.

"So, Samuel? Care to suggest why someone would want you dead?" Walker asked.

Darren shook his head. "Walker."

"Dailon. Call me by that name, Darren. I want you to get to know me, and using my last name creates a distance that shouldn't exist from a man whose dick I held this morning and look forward to having in my mouth later."

"Dailon." Darren corrected. His cock swelled when the professor's cheeks colored a bit.

"There you go. A plus." Dailon smiled. "Now, what were you going to say?"

When Darren moved to pick up another piece of bacon, Samuel took it from him and gave him the orange instead. He then popped the bacon in his mouth and nodded at the orange.

Darren sighed, pulled a section from the orange, and ate it slowly. It wasn't bacon, but it was good. Dailon watched the whole interchange with a soft smile, but it quickly disappeared. His stern demeanor took over as he waited for Darren to respond.

"You were saying?"

"I don't know how to put this. Samuel is an ass." Darren shook his head, laughing when Samuel snorted, and Dailon nodded. "He just is. I don't know what it is about him that attracts both the best people and the worst. He likes to play with them, then he sends them on their way. He's been warned by probably every important member of the pack to cease, but he does it anyway. It could be that someone's had enough."

Samuel sighed. "I've never truly hurt anyone, Darren. What's a little fun?" He sat back, drawing one knee up, somehow looking innocent.

Darren knew he was anything but.

"The problem is, while you may think that it's been just fun, people don't like being discarded and replaced. Sure, they want to enjoy an up-and-coming rock star. Fuck with the guy who turns heads in a crowd. Sometimes that's not enough. They want more. They want to be the center of your attention." His voice had changed at the end, but he couldn't help it.

I want it to be me.

Samuel's smile became wicked, no doubt picking up on Darren's unspoken message. The imp knew him, could easily read him.

Samuel leaned forward then, all cunning and predatory, placed his chin on his fist, eyes bright with mischief. "Do they, Darren?"

Darren's body was on high alert where Samuel was concerned, and the tenderness in his ass was a reminder. He tried to ignore his need, looking away from Samuel.

"Samuel," warned Dailon. "There will be more time for us to play later. I'd like to hear what Darren has to say. I have no doubt the time your family has given us is but a reprieve. Let's work out some ideas here. Besides, don't you have study sessions today?"

Samuel huffed. "Yes, *Daddy*."

Samuel might have meant that sarcastically, but the word had done something for Dailon. His eyes glowed, and his lips curved seductively. "Good boy."

Samuel looked up and glanced at Darren, surprise written in his expression. He turned back to his meal quickly, though the corners of his lips upturned.

It wasn't a secret between him and Samuel that a *Daddy* was something Samuel craved, a dominant man who would care for him, protect him, and keep him. He'd only ever told Darren about this perceived vulnerability. While Samuel enjoyed the company of lovers and playing with them, he never confided in them as he did with Darren.

He looked from Samuel to Dailon and found him watching them closely.

"Darren, continue, please." Dailon wore a sly smile with an amused twinkle in his eyes.

Darren could fall into the depths of those beautiful eyes, which made concentrating difficult. He cleared his throat. "They want Samuel's focus on them, but our guy is fickle and gets bored easily. He doesn't want them forever, just for the moment."

Samuel mumbled something under his breath.

"What was that, Samuel?" Dailon asked.

"I'm not fickle. I couldn't have who I wanted, so I enjoyed who I could. I didn't make any promises to them." Samuel glanced at Darren with a hopeful expression.

Darren reached out an open hand for Samuel to take. Samuel didn't disappoint him. His long fingers were smooth and delicate, but Darren knew the strength there. He squeezed Samuel's hand and smiled when Samuel returned it. "I understand, babe, but that doesn't mean people didn't want those promises desperately enough. This attack could have come from them."

"Could it have been a fan?" Dailon asked. He picked up a mug and drank. Coffee.

Darren imagined sampling the taste from Dailon's lips but focused on the man's words instead. "It's possible. Who can tell? People hurt others for nothing."

Dailon put down the cup and selected a slice of bacon from the center of the table. He nodded, pleased when he took a bite, then leaned over to Darren. "Open."

Darren opened his mouth dutifully, and Dailon fed him the bacon, slipping his fingers inside for Darren to lick clean before removing them.

Dailon licked the same fingers and picked up his cup again. "This is true, but this was also targeted. Some foresight went into it. Like the person was waiting for you to come home, Samuel. Who do you know that might be familiar with your schedule and where you live?"

Samuel shrugged. "I don't know. It had been sort of a rotating doors thing at my place. They'd come. They'd go. No pun intended." His smile was less smirk and more self-disparaging this time. "I don't bring them to my place anymore because . . . it got weird. I thought I was safe on my own grounds, but then this happens."

Dailon nodded. "Your schedule? Do you have anyone other than Darren who knows when you're home and when your classes are?"

"Not really. I have a study group, regular practices with my band, so the people I study with or my bandmates?"

"Which means people who know people. They talk, which makes it harder to pinpoint," Darren speculated.

"But it's a start," Dailon encouraged.

Darren agreed. "We should question them, see if anyone seems suspicious." He was excited now.

Since joining a more established law practice, Darren had less opportunity to do the footwork and knocking on doors. He'd had to rely on others. He missed the up and personal moments where he felt he was making a difference. Milburn and Milburn had investigators and had reminded him that his place was in the courtroom, not at *the home of suspicious characters*. Apparently, it wasn't a good look for someone they were grooming for a chance at partner. He had been instructed to make calls and have others beat the streets. Still, he was eager now, especially where Samuel was concerned, to get some answers.

"Yes, Samuel, love. We will need a list, one as detailed as you can remember about those who might fit the bill here." Dailon wiped his mouth gently. "Let's begin there. You're meeting your group today. Try to feel them out. I will need their names so I can visit them."

"Visit?" Darren asked.

"I have my way of asking questions. One a little closer to home."

"Care to elaborate?" Darren wasn't sure he wanted to hear the answer.

"I can see their dreams, walk in them. I believe it will be helpful here." Dailon rose and began clearing the table. "Now, unless you two are still eating, I'd like to see what we can find out before I trace a line to their dreams."

Samuel looked at Darren. "Dailon, what are you exactly?"

Darren's throat had gone dry, and he was grateful Samuel could ask when he couldn't.

"If I could say human and bring you comfort, I would. But I'm not. I've seen what I look like in the eyes of others as they've slept. I can't completely tell you what I am, Samuel. Or you, Darren. I can say that I've been around for many years, and for the first time in those years, I don't feel alone." Dailon gathered the dishes he'd collected and headed to the kitchen. "A little help is appreciated," he called over his shoulder.

Darren and Samuel stood and gathered the rest of the dishes. Darren felt disconnect and still couldn't speak.

Samuel tried to comfort him. "He may not be one. Different creatures have various abilities."

They took the items into the kitchen and handed them over to Dailon, who put them in the dishwasher.

When they returned to the patio, Samuel continued. "But we don't know, do we? That's what has you spooked."

"I'm not spooked," Darren argued.

"Darren, your hands are shaking, and you look like you're ready to bolt. I get it. I know what you're thinking, baby." Samuel went up to Darren and pulled him against his chest. "There are things about him that remind me of Aiden, but we don't know for sure, and they're not all bad like Keith."

But Keith had been a nightmare, a Sandman just like Aiden. A Sandman could be a monster if left to itself. From what Aiden told him, they could travel the Dreamworld. They were the original influencers on a media larger than life itself. A Sandman could inspire a war, or they could make peace, all with a dream.

Aiden and Keith had been like two sides of a coin. The ability to do good and give to others as a doctor was what Aiden had chosen. Keith had become a manipulator and an abuser.

A Sandman lived forever, but that immortality came at a price. The longer one existed, the more tempting darkness became. They were powerful beings with the ability to blur images, to play with the subconscious mind through daydreams. Whenever the brain wasn't fully engaged, it was an opportunity for a Sandman to slip in and cause mayhem, as Keith had chosen. It could also be the moment a Sandman could heal, as Aiden did. It was a difficult struggle for a creature only known in fairytales.

Choose light or choose darkness? With a Coimeádaí, that choice was made easier.

Darren's torture had ended the day Aiden had eliminated Keith, but the nightmares hadn't stopped. He'd used his fear to live. He savored life, loved his family and friends, laughed, and eventually chosen a career where he could help others. He would not allow Keith to not stop him from living in the light.

But he was a Coimeádaí, destined for a Sandman. He feared there would be another in his life someday, one who would try to claim.

What if that day had come? What was Professor Dalian Walker? The man liked control, liked to position Darren and Samuel in ways that pleased him. In a day, he'd become someone they both needed. He hadn't fucked either of them, but he had wrapped around them.

And his eyes were like Aiden's.

And he could travel the Dreamworld.

Fuck.

Darren's heartbeat raced, but he allowed himself to be held by Samuel. He welcomed the warmth of Samuel's kiss, opened his mouth for his tongue. He was safe.

The thumping he heard in his ears settled down from a pounding drum solo to a gentle, steady beat. He savored Samuel's breath, using it to bring him peace.

Darren heard Dailon return, but he was focused more on Samuel helping him into a chair and settling onto his lap. Samuel's favorite place to sit was often Darren's legs, where he would recline against Darren's chest and let Darren pet him. It was more for Darren than for Samuel. It was something he did when he knew Darren needed comfort. This time, Samuel's lips and tongue were busy, along with his wandering hands sliding down Darren's chest. Samuel reached around Darren's waist and tugged at his shirt to touch his skin.

Darren moaned into Samuel's mouth, smiling when he felt strong hands touch his shoulders.

"You are beautiful together," Dailon said. "Like a work of art. My sweet possessions." He reached down and twisted Darren's nipples.

The pain was sharp, and Darren's cock, already hard from Samuel's kisses, woke up and took notice.

"Like that, Darren? I'd love to see you stretched out, my lovely living sacrifice, there to be pleasured. Do you like a little pain, Darren? I know Samuel does. He begs for it."

Samuel kissed Darren harder, shifting to rub his cock along Darren's belly. His teeth nipped at Darren's lips, and Dailon twisted Darren's nipples again.

Darren came like a greedy teenager, the shocks rumbling through him. Samuel followed him.

They were a mess, but Darren had loved every second of it.

"Now, we need to get you cleaned up and back to your car," Dailon interrupted. "I'm certain I received an assessment on my vehicle through my insurance agency."

"That was fast," Darren managed after catching his breath.

"A little encouragement never hurts. They wanted to get it done. I simply aided. Now, I have a few errands to run. Have something to say, Samuel?"

Samuel, whose face rested in the crook of Darren's neck, rolled his head to look at Dailon. "I don't want to leave."

Darren glanced at Dailon, who smiled, his eyes betraying what Darren was also feeling. He didn't want to leave, either. There was something about Dailon that scared the ever-loving hell out of Darren. But rather than pushing away, he was drawn to the man like the proverbial moth to a flame.

Dailon trailed a hand down Samuel's back and crouched low. "How about you come back tonight, both of you? Stay with me. Let me take care of you."

Samuel wrapped his legs around Darren. "Please, Darren?"

Darren wanted to hesitate, should have thought of reasons why this was a bad idea. But his gaze was on Dailon, who eagerly watched and waited for an answer.

The only one Darren could give was, "Yes."

Chapter Nine

Samuel sat in the library with his study group in a fresh set of clothes that were not sticky wet from cum. He didn't know these people, could barely remember their names, but Dailon had asked him so he would try.

He asked me, so I'm doing this.

Or was it demanded? Ordered? Professor Dailon Walker made him want to do what he told him.

The night before had been ecstasy, Samuel so deep in Darren's ass he could feel his heartbeat, and the professor had what had to be four fingers shoved in his hole. Dailon had applied just the right amount of pressure to that special spot for stars to go off.

Samuel wanted that again. Only next time, Dailon's dick could replace those fingers. It was crazy. He'd hoped for what had happened. Had never dreamed it would be like this.

"Samuel, you normally have a good grasp of how we include the community angle. What do you think?"

Marly. Carly. What the fuck is her name?

"Uh, let me think. We could host an event. Maybe get some key people involved. The sororities and fraternities are always looking for a cause. If we make this a genuine thing, it would be sure to earn points."

"Yeah, man. I could use some points," the girl said. "My mom says if I don't get off my ass in my classes, she's going to make me work in the family restaurant. No free ride."

Marly. Carly. Kate? She looks like a Kate. The girl nodded, and Billy Bob high-fived her. *He could be a Billy Bob.*

"While they like the idea, where the fuck could we have an event? None of us have a place for this." A curly-haired boy said.

Samuel had been planning to fuck the guy later that week. He was an angry, pouty thing, and Samuel enjoyed playing with them the most. In the end, they typically begged to stay but could be counted on for some seriously intense orgasms. But, no, not now. He had his guys for that, his Double Ds. Darren's hole, and maybe one day Dailon's, were the only ones he wanted to squeeze his dick inside.

Focus. Focus. Answer angry boy's question.

"Tim. Peter. Jack."

"Richard. My name is Richard, which you should know by now, but whatever."

Look at the way Richard . . . Wait, wasn't the nickname for Richard Dick? Samuel choked his laugh off in a snort. He could call him Dick, right? Didn't using nicknames count as building relationships or something?

"So, Dick, a place is what you're thinking? A venue?"

Dick rolled his eyes. "Yeah. It's great making all these plans, working on these details, but what we need is a location. One where the professor could visit and note our progress. If we impress him, I'm sure our final grades are a win-win all around."

"Smart thinking there. I like it," Samuel commended.

Dick simply nodded, but his expression reflected his pleasure at the praise.

The last to speak was the guy currently finishing a sandwich, which technically wasn't permitted inside the library. But then there were a lot of things considered forbidden in this library that Samuel had ignored a time or two himself for a pleasurable outcome.

"Yeah," the guy mumbled around a full mouth.

Oh, great thoughts there.

"Thank you." Samuel just barely managed to not laugh out

loud.

"Biff. Name's Biff."

"Not that you should know that one, either," Dick commented.

Samuel grinned and must have flashed a hint of teeth, because Dick blanched for a moment and took a step back.

"Hey, maybe once we figure out the location, could you do a song or two? That would be too cool and well-received." Kate said.

Samuel was sure her name was Kate.

"Well, Kate,"

"Barbara."

He hadn't missed the collective roll of eyes from all around. "Yes, Barbara. I guess that could work. My guys would love that."

They will fucking hate it.

Because while it allowed them to play a venue, he'd told them they would take a break. Maybe they would agree to only one or two songs? Or he could just do it himself. Guitar and a stool, right. Could use a microphone. It depended on the acoustics of the place they chose.

But where?

"But I'm thinking maybe I could do a solo thing, just me."

"Oh wow! That would totally work." Barbara was eager, those big brown eyes shining with excitement. "It would be more intimate. If you chose songs that fit with the cause, there's no way people wouldn't donate. You have like a magical voice and everything."

The cause they'd chosen was youth homelessness, which was on a list of five other possibilities Dr. Whit had offered. Samuel wasn't sure why the others had agreed. Still, he knew how important homeless youths, particularly gay youths, were to Peter, Kristoff's nephew. Peter worked hard to make sure lost children had a place to go, somewhere to turn. Samuel remembered the stories Peter told of those too vulnerable to fend for themselves with horrible outcomes, human trafficking being one of them.

If they could stop that by taking a class assignment for socio-economics to the next level and make that real, something that could honestly make a difference? Why the hell not?

"So, where is this thing going to be?" Dick asked.

Now, that. Samuel had some ideas. He couldn't wait to tell him.

"You said what?" Kristoff Dumanovsky was not pleased. "What in the name of the Goddess Moon were you thinking?"

Samuel had finished classes early. He hadn't seen Dailon waiting around for him, but Darren was there, ready to take him home.

They were quiet on the ride, Darren glancing over at him and back to the road. He'd wanted to tease him, but it looked like he needed some time. He could give him that, but he refused to let him dwell. Dwelling was like riding a rocking horse. It didn't get a person anywhere, and he wanted this thing with Darren to go somewhere.

The night before had been a turning point. Samuel refused to go back to the way things had been. So he'd waited for a bit, then reached over and ran his index finger along Darren's wrist. Darren had sighed, then turned his hand over, and Samuel had clasped it. They'd driven the rest of the way in silence, holding hands, quiet and together.

It was when they'd arrived at Samuel's house that they had found a volatile Kristoff Dumanovsky standing in the doorway with his arms crossed, waiting. The man was too beautiful for his own good.

What? I have eyes.

His grandfather was happy. His people were happy. Even the vampires who had taken up residence on pack lands celebrated Jeremiah Tolliver and his alpha mate. Samuel remembered joining in the hunt. It had gone sideways, but in the end, all was well. Kristoff didn't look too happy as he stood there glaring at Samuel.

Good times.

"Oh, so they called you, then?" Samuel knew Barbara had been only too happy to help after he'd expressed that his grandparent's grounds would be lovely to hold the event. He'd told her he just didn't know if he could ask himself. He was such a shy person at times . . . at least he had acted the part.

Samuel observed the crease in Kristoff's brow, the frustration so vivid he wished he could paint. Kristoff's customary black and gunmetal gray clothes complimented the fire blazing from his eyes.

"It's a great way to promote the pack," he added. "And Peter would appreciate the purpose."

"He would? That was your reasoning, and not to punish me for leaving?" Kristoff stared him down, waiting.

No one could say Kristoff wasn't observant. He knew people and could read them easily. It was a talent that helped him execute his vital role as the alpha mate, working to help the alpha lead the pack. He met with the people, arranged the events, all things he'd done in the past without the title. Now in his official capacity—one he hadn't readily accepted—he did that much and more.

If Samuel were a bit salty, it was because Kristoff had always been there for him, and then he wasn't. Samuel was the wayward brat to Kristoff, but his censure had always come with love and protection. Kristoff had been the one to step between Samuel and his father and challenge Samuel but never believe less of him.

Samuel had felt abandoned when Kristoff had left the pack. So what else could he do but retaliate in small ways? Just enough to create burrs under the alpha mates' skin. A tiny twist here or there.

For example, telling his study group the best place for the

event was on pack grounds, or as he'd told them, his grandfather's land. After he'd described the massive house, the rolling hills, and the ponds spaced about the grounds, they were sold.

He'd suggested Barbara call to make it official. It would be more professional if one of them contacted the family and spoke to the right hand of the Tolliver lands. It would impress the professor and all that if they each performed a task lending this the authenticity it needed.

Samuel had even provided her the phone number. The only thing better would have been watching Kristoff answer the call himself.

But this right here was close to perfect.

"Moi?" Samuel said, pointing at himself for effect.

"Yes, you *soplyak*."

"Am I truly a jerk, Alpha Mate? I was just trying to get us some great exposure in helping Peter's cause. I'm sure it won't be a problem. It is why you're here, after all, to care for the pack."

Kristoff's glare was magnificent.

"You look very nice, Alpha Mate. Going somewhere?"

Kristoff had on a dress shirt the color of steel and well-fitting black slacks that hugged his wide frame and accented his narrow waist. A simple chain with a J hanging from the center that sparkled in diamonds draped his neck. He'd refused a ring, but Samuel's grandfather had insisted on a token, a sign of their promise. It was a slipknot of sorts that would fall to accommodate the size of Kristoff's wolf. It would never leave him, always a sign of to whom he belonged.

It was something Samuel had always hoped to give Darren. And now? Now he thought about Dailon. Would Dailon wear his token? Would he be able to claim both Darren and Dailon?

His smile must have shifted into something warmer, because Kristoff looked at him oddly.

"I have somewhere to be, yes." Kristoff frowned. "If I am to be ready for this event that must happen next week, there are people I must meet, calls to be made as well as organize. However, I am able to reschedule, especially as I have also been tasked with speaking to you once again about your safety." He lifted his head and scented the air, then glared at Darren and back at Samuel. "Explain."

Samuel huffed. "I don't have to explain anything to you."

"You will explain why there are multiple scents on you. Darren, who I know well enough, and the other we only met last night. You've fucked or been fucked by both." He breathed in again. "And the other? He is not human. Have you even showered?"

At least twice, but that would mean nothing to Kristoff. The alpha mate used that nose of his to hunt down his intended targets without fail. Tactful, though? That he would never be.

"Crude, Kristoff."

"Honest, Samuel Dimitri Cillian Tolliver."

His entire name. Touché.

Samuel's wolf growled inside at the challenge, and Darren squeezed his arm tightly. Samuel was instantly centered, the need to prove himself to Kristoff vanishing into thin air. Instead, his wolf huffed, wanting more than ever to scent Darren, to mark him more than he had that night.

"Kristoff, as you are leaving and we plan to be here this evening, there will be more than enough time for us to talk. Samuel?" Darren spoke calmly.

That smooth-as-silk voice of Darren's encouraged Samuel to nod easily.

Kristoff smiled his almost trademark barely-there smile, his eyes warming as he looked at Darren. It hadn't always been that way. At one point, Kristoff had held great disdain for humans, feeling they were useless, but Danny had found a means of warming his way into that icy heart. He'd earned

Kristoff's respect years ago. And when Danny had moved Darren and his grandmother onto pack lands, Kristoff had made room for more humans.

"We can always count on you, Darren, to help our young one keep a civil tongue," Kristoff said.

Samuel hissed. "I'd like to show you exactly what I can do with this tongue."

"Would you?" Darren asked.

There was a sliver of ice in Darren's tone that made Samuel's dick rise and take notice. He was breathless for a moment, then he shivered.

"Yes, Samuel? Anything to say there? Human got your tongue?" Kristoff's laughter faded as he turned to walk away. "I've never heard him speechless before, Darren. I'll talk to you later. The event is for this Friday, which you somehow managed to set up for the night before a full moon. When you fuck up, my son, you do it royally."

My son. Not brat, not even the Russian equivalent soplyak.

"Did you hear him?" Samuel mused.

"Yes, I did. And while I know how much that means to you, no more quips about your tongue on anyone else other than me or Dailon."

Samuel smiled. It seemed they both had accepted there would be three of them. It was so fast this feeling, this need for the three of them. It had felt incredible when he'd finally had his first true taste of Darren, his dick deep in his ass with those tight ass muscles squeezing him hard.

He'd dreamed about it. Hell, he wanted it now, but Kristoff had called him his *son,* and that was where his brain was stuck.

Well, that and thinking of the three of them together again.

"Samuel?" Darren was waiting for his answer.

Samuel smiled. His thoughts had been everywhere but his comment. "Never, Darren. I will never touch another with my tongue or anything else as long as I have my Double Ds."

Darren raised a brow. "Double Ds?"

"Darren and Dailon, Double Ds."

Darren laughed softly, and Samuel wanted to feel the sound against his lips, dip his tongue inside, and sample his flavor again.

"I want that too, Samuel."

"You can read my thoughts?"

"No, baby. I can read how much you want me all over your face. I want you to have me again. Been feeling your dick in my ass all day. But I don't think we're getting any alone time right now. I think I hear someone in your home right now."

"Samuel, you may be able to talk to Kristoff later, but you better get your little minxy ass in this house right the fuck now."

"Mom?"

Chapter Ten

Darren almost laughed at Samuel's reaction to his mother's voice. Samuel and his mother could have been twins, both beautiful and equally dangerous. As defiant as Samuel tried to be, Shelly would not be bested, especially by her own son.

You can't get the best of Shelly Tolliver, Sprite of Western Winds.

Samuel might have power, could easily bend nature to do his building, but his mother could wield that power and make it her own.

She was terrifying, and right now, she was sitting at the table, no child anywhere. Typically, she carried one of her young with another following her. At last count, his siblings numbered eleven, but she loved fiercely, protectively, and gave her all to each one. To see her empty-handed meant she'd arrived at Samuel's home with a purpose.

"An bhfuil aon smaoineamh agat cad atá á dhéanamh agat?" Shelly asked in a stern tone.

Darren only caught a word or two of what she'd said. *Idea. Doing*. He might have lived here on these lands for years before he left to get his law degree, but he'd never fully grasped all the languages people spoke. He could probably figure it out, though. He was fairly certain he'd heard those words thrown at Samuel in one language or another as long as he'd known him.

"It depends on what you think I'm doing, and English, please, Mom. My mate needs to understand what we're discussing." Samuel exuded happiness, no matter how non-chalant he tried to appear.

And Darren was certain Shelly could detect it.

Shelly turned and pierced him with a look, and he counted himself blessed that he was like family. That might be what would save him from being dragged physically from the room by a sudden windstorm. He'd seen it happen before.

Her glare turned to a half-smile. "I love Darren, and while I'm glad you two are finally of the same mind, there is a great deal more happening here."

Samuel often wished his father spent more time with him, saw him as capable. He also wished his mother didn't see him quite as clearly. Well, there was no way he was getting that wish this day. He huffed a sigh of resignation. "I'm thirsty. I thought maybe I would fix a drink."

"Are you? Well, I am, too," Shelly said. "And I bet Darren could use a drink himself. He seems a tad wrung dry. A glass of wine for me, maybe water for Darren while you're at it." Her hair swayed gently in the quiet of the room, evidence of her harnessed power mixed with fear for her eldest.

"Yes, ma'am. I would love a glass of water. Thank you," Darren said. "Samuel, I believe we should talk to your mother. Thank you for dropping by, Shelly." Acceptance would go a long way to tempering the coming storm.

Shelly's hair settled softly on her shoulders, and she smiled. "Thank you, Darren. I can't tell you how often I've thanked She who gave us life that you were here for Samuel. You just have a way."

Darren didn't miss Samuel's dramatic eye-roll. He was tempted to smack Samuel's sweet ass when he stormed off noisily to get his mother a drink. Instead, he turned to face Shelly, who watched him knowingly.

"Yes. *Déanfaidh tú*. You'll do. Now, tell me about this other one who ferried you off last night."

You'll do, she says.

Darren smiled.

Shelly settled in and waited, obviously not leaving until she got some answers. But where could they start? Though Darren mentioned someone possibly wanting revenge for some perceived transgression Samuel committed, he couldn't confirm his thoughts. Would telling Shelly his thoughts even be a good idea?

He did his best to watch Samuel, which he had to admit was self-serving. Even now, he gazed at his beautiful Samuel moving around in his bright as hell kitchen. The clash of colors seemed to work, each wall claiming a variant of the rainbow, the blue chrome he'd used in the fixtures, along with his bright yellow fiftyish refrigerator. Add in the fact that the table and chairs where Darren and Shelly waited to be served were grass green, completing the tableau, and it was like being outside on a bright spring day.

Samuel's need for color was only one of the reasons Darren loved the man. And he did love Samuel, had, it seemed like forever.

He was tired of running from where he belonged. Darren wanted Samuel for himself, and he wanted him with Dailon. They just needed to see if Dailon knew they were a forever thing and not just for the moment.

"Waiting." Shelly strummed her fingers on the table.

Samuel sighed and pulled two wine glasses from his cabinet. Their style was typical Samuel, with stems of blown glass and flames running over and around them. They were as stunning as the man that carried them.

Darren licked his lips, and Samuel smiled at him shyly. He wasn't sure he'd ever seen that look before.

"Eye fuck later, you two. Talk." Shelly pointed a bright yellow fingernail toward Samuel's wine rack. "Oh, and Samuel, I wanted to try the chocolate truffle one. It's already chilled."

Samuel shook his head and laughed. "Presumptuous

much, Mom?"

"I only wanted you to be prepared," Shelly responded with equal saccharine.

"Oh, of course." Samuel opened the refrigerator door and retrieved the wine Shelly requested, then bent to kiss her on the cheek. "Anything for the best mother in the world."

And that was another reason Darren loved Samuel. For all his brattiness and his need to prove something to the pack, he loved his mother deeply and even stepped in to watch his siblings on occasion. He would do anything for her, for them, and for Connor. He'd argued with them, with anyone who wanted him to be different—more pack less rock star—but he loved them all. The shredding of his two selves as he struggled against who he wanted to be and who they wanted him to be was what made life hard for everyone involved.

In his way, Darren had tried speaking to them. Tried to get them to see what they were doing and what Samuel needed. But he was human. Apparently more human than Danny, which didn't go a long way in proving his say mattered. At least not in the eyes of the pack.

Shelly's eyes glowed with happiness, and she tugged Samuel's hair. "Silly boy, now spill."

As Samuel described meeting Dailon, Darren sat back, drinking his water, which Samuel would automatically refill without missing a beat.

Samuel always did that for him, took care of him. When he was frustrated, Samuel would sit in his lap and allow him to pet him. When Samuel thought he was too focused on his studies and later working himself too hard, he found a way to distract him, from dragging him off to go ice skating to shifting into one of his forms so they could go on a chase. When his grandmother was sick, and he worried he would lose her, Samuel never left his side.

Samuel was always there for him.

It finally clicked in Darren's head. Samuel loved him as much as he loved Samuel. He probably always had.

I've been an idiot. Wasted so much time.

Not again. Not for them and not for Dailon.

"So, where is he now? This professor?" Shelly asked. "Your father is going to want to know. He is curious why on a night when this stranger brings you home, someone takes a shot at you."

Darren nodded. "I understand what you're saying, Shelly, but neither of us feels like Dailon had anything to do with last night other than helping us to find a safe place to stay the night."

"You are safer on pack grounds," a voice boomed into the room. Jeremiah Tolliver stood in the doorway, his presence swallowing the air in the room as alphas sometimes did.

"Alpha," Shelly said, smiling. "You should have a seat, shouldn't he, Samuel?"

Darren could see Samuel running through responses, none of them any that would help the current situation.

"Samuel," Darren warned in a soft tone.

Samuel glanced at him. Darren smiled, and Samuel melted.

"Of course, Mom. Grandfather, would you like something to drink?" Samuel's tone remained respectful.

Darren shifted uncomfortably, the soft words a reminder of Samuel's cock in his ass.

Shelly sniffed, hiding a smile in her glass as she took a sip. Maybe Darren hadn't been as discreet as he thought.

Darren, shifting again, chose to watch the grandfather and grandson interaction instead. He noticed the alpha lift a brow in surprise.

Jeremiah nodded. "That I would, *grá*."

Samuel couldn't quite hide his pleasure at pleasing Jeremiah. "I have wine, juice, uhm, anything. Coffee?"

"My mate has denied me coffee. Says it's not good for my

wolf." Jeremiah's glare challenged each of them to comment. "I would like a cup of coffee, but that man knows everything I do."

"And it makes you happy, Alpha." Shelly nodded. "Kristoff is good for you and your wolf. Him returning to the pack has done nothing but bless us, even if some would challenge him at every turn."

"So no coffee then," Samuel said. "I won't be the one to answer to him for that one. I pick my battles."

"Battles that shouldn't happen. You know my mate loves you," Jeremiah argued.

Samuel sighed. "Yes, I know."

"It was my fault, not his for his leaving. I behaved foolishly, too caught up in my grief and darkness to see the light that Kristoff offered me. Forgive him, grá, and let him give you what you need."

Samuel turned away. "So, orange juice. Orange juice should be good."

Jeremiah sighed. "Yes, I can have that at least but not too much. The sugar is bad. Ha! I'm going to live at least two or three hundred more years. Why does it matter how much sugar I have or coffee I drink?"

Is Jeremiah Tolliver pouting? Would anyone notice if I recorded this to share later?

"Kristoff wants the rest of your years together to be healthy ones, Grandfather. He loves you, and if you love him the way I see you do, you'll listen. I may have my issues with him right now, but my mother is right. Kristoff being here is what is best for you and best for the pack."

"Ah. Look at you, being an adult," Jeremiah teased.

And that was all it took for Samuel to immediately shut down.

"No, son. I didn't mean it like that."

Shelly shook her head.

"How exactly did you mean it, Alpha?" Ice had crept into

Samuel's tone.

Darren reached out and pulled Samuel to him. "Sit. Listen. Let's get through this so we can find Dailon." He slid his hand up and down Samuel's back, petting him gently, easing his tension.

"Conner is checking into the shooting, combing the grounds," Jeremiah said. "His men saw tracks leading in. The person had climbed a tree. Looks like that's where he took point."

"So, there's no question of Samuel being a target," Darren needed that confirmed, though he was hopeful it was otherwise.

Even with Kristoff and Connor's hypervigilance, an occasional adventurous idiot slipped through. Rather than being torn apart by the phalanx of guards constantly checking the perimeter, trespassers were typically dragged to the main house and arrested. There were times when more extreme measures were required against an intruder, and Darren didn't feel any remorse for them. He understood how vital it was to keep the people that lived here safe. For a person to drive onto the grounds and climb a tree to shoot at a car parked near Samuel's home, there could be no mistake of the intended target.

"Or Dailon," Jeremiah suggested.

Darren shook his head. "I don't agree with that. Samuel didn't even know Dailon before yesterday when the two met. And last night, there was no trouble at his home."

"His home, yes. Interesting that." Jeremiah said. "Well then, since you're not sure if this could be related to the stranger who has become a part of my grandson's and now your life, then maybe all three of you should stay here."

"So you can keep an eye on him," Samuel growled.

"Samuel, I know what you think, but let me promise you, boy, I have nothing but your safety in mind. First, you are my own. Part of my line. Second, you are a part of my pack as you will always be." Jeremiah raised his hand. "Wait, let me speak, grá. I'm no perfect man. I make mistakes. Last night in speaking to you, I allowed my feelings to get ahead of me. You are my heart, Samuel. Are you different? Yes. But we all are in one way or another. I love every part of you, from the crest of your wild mane to your booted feet. You're mine, you hear?" Jeremiah slammed his fist on the table, his bracelets ringing around his wrists.

"Yes, sir. Yes, Alpha." Samuel spoke in a quiet tone with a sparkle of tears shining in his eyes.

"Now, I don't expect you to understand every last thought of mine, but I need you to know I must protect you and mine. It's why I exist other than to love Kristoff to the end of my time. Sometimes I forget to say what's important. You're important to me. I promise you, every bit of you."

Jeremiah reached over and pulled Samuel out of Darren's lap and into his arms. "Every bit of you."

When Samuel laid his head on his grandfather's shoulder and allowed himself to be held, Darren felt the happiness in his soul.

The two men were quiet for a moment, and then Samuel wiped his eyes. "You can't have coffee, but I do have some tea. No caffeine. It's still great, though."

Jeremiah suspiciously cleared his throat, and Darren pretended not to notice the alpha's eyes were wet as well.

"Aye, that would be welcome, boy. Can't see Kristoff denying me that."

While Samuel prepared the tea, they talked about the upcoming event and what it would mean to Peter. Samuel described his study group members while Darren listened carefully to see if any details might lead them to a possible suspect. Shelly offered ideas they hadn't considered, maybe someone looking to challenge Jeremiah's leadership and stir up trouble. There was always a possibility someone wasn't happy with the changes Jeremiah had brought to the pack. Especially his human son, the vampires living on the grounds, and other humans who'd moved onto the lands as well.

While it was possible, Darren didn't think that was it. The people were happy. He hadn't met a person, wolf or otherwise, that wasn't grateful to have the alpha bonded with his alpha mate. Those he'd spoken to would fight for their leaders at a moment's notice. The pack was at peace, and while there were conflicts, they were easily resolved. It was the reason he'd felt safe bringing his grandmother to live her final days here. It was why she was buried on pack grounds. This was home. It was a sanctuary for all who lived here.

"No, Mom. I don't think that's it either. But I have no other ideas." Samuel noticed Jeremiah's cup was empty and held up the teapot. "More, grandfather?"

Samuel the caretaker.

There are layers to my . . . Friend? Lover? Mate? Mate. Darren sighed.

Samuel was immediately at his side, his palm beneath his chin lifting his head to peer into his eyes. "You okay there?"

Darren became completely lost within Samuel's honey golden eyes. His touch was warm and gentle, his need to take care of Darren shining for all to see.

Darren needed what Samuel offered. He would no longer deny himself. "Yes, baby. Just a little tired. Maybe a nap?"

Shelly nodded. "Of course. Alpha, can you walk with me to the house? I will probably need an extra hand or two to capture a few butterflies."

Jeremiah laughed knowingly. "Yes, I could do that." He stood. "Samuel, you take care of Darren there. He rushed to be here for you. And from the look of you two, I don't think sleeping is what happened last night. We'll talk another time.

Let me help your mother with her butterflies."

"Mom?" Samuel said, but his gaze was glued on Darren.

"Baby, I'm fairly certain a nap is not the only thing your mate needs. I'd rather not have a front-row seat to that show." Shelly took Jeremiah's elbow, and the two parted quickly.

Darren parted his lips for Samuel's gentle kiss. "Fuck me," he murmured.

Samuel shivered. "Oh, yes, darling."

Chapter Eleven

Dailon sat at his desk and prepared his lesson for the next evening's class. He looked at his phone, the desire to call Darren and Samuel great. They were so open to him, so beautiful in their submission. He ached for it now, but he had work to do.

His car had been repaired, not that he'd given it much thought. The window was an easy fix. What worried him more was what could have happened. It wasn't like he would have died, but to possibly have lost Samuel when he'd only just found him, and his tie with Darren, was too much.

His mothers had spoken to him last year, promising that in their shared vision, he would meet those he needed. At that point, he'd given up on having someone, anyone. No matter who he chose for an evening of pleasure, it was never enough. They shared a moment where his company was excited about the thrill but never the long haul. He had started telling himself he didn't need more.

He did, though. He needed someone who begged for his touch, who screamed and still ask for more. He craved the person who could accept the dark side of himself, the part of him he'd chosen to embrace years ago.

When he'd asked his mothers how he would know, they were their mysterious selves and only said he would know. Their warning?

Know thyself.

First, no one spoke in such terms anymore. Second, Dailon knew exactly who he was, if not what.

Dailon pushed back away from his desk. He'd be lying to himself if he thought he could accomplish any work. Not when what he truly hungered for were the two beautiful men he pictured in his bed . . . repeatedly.

His mind replayed the visual loop. Stuffing almost his whole fist in Samuel's ass while Samuel fucked Darren. Swallowing Darren's cock while he twisted his balls. Sharing the taste of Darren's seed with Samuel and licking the marks along Samuel's neck while Darren knelt behind him and ate Samuel's hole.

He'd barely slept the last few days, remembering the three of them in bed together.

If I want them so much, what am I waiting on to have them?

Fear, both irrational and completely useless but entirely real, overwhelmed him.

Know thyself.

Darren and Samuel would change his life, his world.

Am I ready for that?

He'd thought about traveling in their dreams, visiting them, but he'd held back. Refused. It would take only moments to find the threads to get to them, but what would he see? What would he discover?

Dailon took a breath and returned to typing. He'd nearly given up again when he heard a knock on his door.

Surprised, he looked up. He sent out his awareness to prod the psyche of the person on the other side and took a deep breath when one remained closed to him, but the other he already knew well.

"Come in, Darren and Samuel." His voice held more confidence than he felt.

There they stood, and suddenly hiding in the guise of working and responsibilities didn't matter anymore.

What he needed were the two men who had entered the room.

Samuel wore a loose-fitting blue shirt with a satiny sheen

and a pair of canary yellow jeans that looked painted on. His hair was tied back rather than falling around his face. Darren was wearing a short-sleeved green t-shirt and chinos, his hair freshly cut. They were mouth-watering, and Dailon said good-bye to his reservations immediately.

"We've come to take you to lunch, then home." Samuel's eyes held a hint of challenge.

"Are you asking or telling me, Samuel?" Dailon stood and slowly rounded the desk. He enjoyed the way Samuel's eyes widened that much more, taking all of him in. Dailon wasn't a small man. He was tall, wide, and his size often intimidated others. For Samuel, that might be a challenge, one he wouldn't be able to resist.

Dailon loved the deep breath Samuel took, obviously inhaling his scent. The darting of his tongue across his plump lip made him itch to shove the pretty man to his knees and show him how he wanted his cock sucked.

"Whatever would make that happen, Dailon. We've missed you. At first, we thought giving you some time to come to us would be good, but then we realized you were taking too long." Samuel moved closer.

"We?" Dailon asked, welcoming Samuel's touch, sliding up his ribs and across his nipples, making him ache deliciously. He moaned when Samuel bit his flesh, then looked at Darren, watching them with a heated look. "Is it we, Darren?"

Darren nodded. "I'm the one who told Samuel we couldn't wait anymore."

"Did you? Well, why are you standing over there? Come here. Touch me."

Darren didn't hesitate. He strode to Dailon, who kissed him and savored the taste of lips he'd missed. The kiss was long and passionate, teeth clacking against teeth with need.

Dailon lifted his head and looked at Darren intently. "Tonight, it will be my cock in your ass."

Darren's noises were decadent when Dailon reached around to the curve of his ass and slid a finger down his crease.

"Right there is where I'm going to put my seed. Going to fuck you raw with just the slightest bit of lube, so you feel me for days to come. You want that, Darren? Want me to own your ass?"

"I do," Samuel interjected. "I want you to own his ass. Then I want you to own mine. Can you do that, Dailon?"

Dailon's head fell back when Samuel palmed his dick and squeezed.

"You want us now, don't you, Dailon?" Samuel murmured low and sexy. "Been thinking of us on our knees worshipping your dick, our asses in the air for the taking. Or were you remembering your fingers in my ass as I fucked Darren?"

Samuel initiated a kiss, his wicked tongue doing carnal things to Dailon's mouth. For just a moment, Dailon envisioned his ass being owned by both of these men, which wasn't his typical choice. Dailon fucked the men he enjoyed. He didn't get fucked.

He gathered the men close, not wanting to let go. "I need one of you on the floor now. Darren, lock the door. One of you will be on the floor with your mouth wrapped around my dick. The other gets to swallow. I don't care who goes first."

Samuel moaned. "I want to go first."

Darren turned toward the door, locking it.

"Darren, take your dick out. Good. Let me see that. Stroke it nice and slow. I want it out the entire time Samuel sucks me. Samuel, I'm going to stuff my dick down your throat now. I want to see your head move. You won't be able to breathe, but I have you. This is what I need right now. You will give me that, won't you, baby?"

"Goddess Moon, yes. I will. I love seeing you like this, all shiny with need." Samuel knelt gracefully, the blue of his shirt catching the light, making him look otherworldly.

"You are a beautiful creature. I've been thinking about our night together. I almost called you both. Now you're here, and I can't stop myself from having more of you." Dailon stepped forward then. "So beautiful. I have no idea how Darren waited for you. The moment I saw you, I wanted you. I don't think I can let you go."

Bottomless brown eyes looked up as Dailon slid his hand along Samuel's chin and then up to his lips. He slipped his thumb inside, running it over Samuel's white teeth. "I want to see your fangs. Give me that. I want them to slide along my dick while you suck me. I want my blood over your lips, inside your mouth. Can you give me that, beautiful one?"

Samuel opened his mouth, dropping his fangs.

"So beautiful and sharp. I can't wait to feel the tips along my length. Open wide. There you go, beautiful. Wider."

Dailon placed the crown of his dick on Samuel's tongue. "Taste me." He smiled when Samuel obeyed, licking gently. "You have quite a talented tongue there. Darren, our boy feels exquisite. Let him taste you."

Darren's gaze roamed Samuel's body.

"Yes, you want this. You wouldn't have that big monster of yours out if you didn't. Let him taste you, get you slick. It'll be easier to slide through your fists."

Darren stepped over, dick in hand, sighing when Samuel took it in his mouth, or as much as he could get of it. It was a lovely piece of interaction.

Dailon groaned at the sight. "Get it sloppy and wet, Samuel. Excellent. Now, back to me. Darren, go back to tugging. Yes. Look at me while I shove my dick down Samuel's tight throat like his sweet ass. Had no idea I was getting this today. You are the answer to a prayer."

Dailon put his hands on either side of Samuel's head and slid in. "Ah." The mix of pain and pleasure was everything he needed. He thrust into Samuel's mouth, fucking his dick down his throat, enjoying the sharp pain of his fangs. "Let me check." He looked down to watch the length of his dick moving beneath the musculature of Samuel's throat.

He pulled back. "Breathe quickly."

Samuel did as instructed, then grunted when Dailon shoved back in. Dailon rocked back and forth, taking his pleasure. He knew exactly when the saliva inside Samuel's mouth combined with his blood. He felt his energy slide out, seeking Samuel and then reaching for Darren. It was both of them. Whatever he needed, he would only have it with them both.

It was scary, but he was too focused on the way Samuel was taking him, the way his tongue ran over his dick, and the tightness of his throat.

He felt it then, the churning in his balls, and opened eyes he hadn't realized he'd closed. His power was upon him, and though it was hard, he pulled himself out of Samuel's mouth and growled at Darren, "Get on your knees. I need you to swallow my seed. Samuel, help him."

Samuel struggled to stand and wiped his mouth, blood, saliva, and probably pre-come on his chin. "Darren."

Darren seemed lost in sensation but allowed Samuel to help him fall to his knees in front of Dailon.

"There you are, my beautiful one. Open wide." When Darren obeyed immediately, his hands still pulling and tugging his dick, Dailon shoved into his hot wet mouth. "Swallow." It took one thrust, one swallow, and Dailon was pouring himself down Darren's throat, feeding him. "Next time, Samuel. Right now, Darren, suck harder. Need this. Need to know I'm inside you, all of me."

Samuel ran his hands over Darren's shoulder when he struggled for air. "Calm, baby. Be calm. Good. It's so good, right? I had a taste, and it was light and music. Like a drug."

Dailon smiled and continued to fill Darren with seed. He shook and trembled and then nearly fell on top of Darren when it became too much. "Yes," he encouraged. "Get every drop."

Darren hummed, his mouth popping when Dailon withdrew. Darren licked him then, his eyes dazed.

"Good job. So lovely," Dailon said as he touched Darren tenderly. "Now, lunch. That would be good. You can tell me what I've missed."

Dailon liked Callie's, a place he had frequented in the Highlands as long as he'd lived in Louisville, not that he knew how long that had been. His life had begun the day he'd met his mothers, after all. Callie's had been one of the first pleasures they shared with him, a warm meal and clothing. A full belly and safety.

Callie's was still very much the same as it had been years past. Mirrors decorated the walls, allowing Dailon the opportunity to see himself at any angle . . . or the two men he sat with. Darren looked over the menu, his lips still swollen from Dailon using him earlier. Samuel's lips were as well. Dailon was happy, satisfied. It was a feeling he'd lacked for years, one he never wanted to lose.

The look of completion on them both? Dailon had done that. He loved looking at the aftermath, the evidence of his ardor.

The waitress arrived to take their order, and Darren looked at him. "I'm not very hungry. I'm full, actually, so I'll just have water."

Dailon smiled knowingly. "I'd like for you to try their sweet potato pie, at least. It's one of my favorites. Taste it."

At the word taste, Samuel shifted noticeably, and Dailon touched his wrist. "Soon."

Samuel rolled his eyes.

Dailon laughed. "Now, answer the woman so we can talk."

Samuel rattled off his order, and the waitress turned to Dailon. He ordered his meal and the waitress walked away with a nod.

Dailon touched Darren's cheek gently. "You are beautiful beyond measure. Thank you for honoring me."

He sounded old, ancient, even to his own ears. It had been a problem in his youth, the inability to sound like those around him. Often, he'd felt like he was from a different time. He treasured more than his peers, who played games and chased the next high. He had always been more focused, living with purpose as he did now.

His mother, Adrianna, had told him he'd come to them wet and cold, lost, their gift. From the moment he'd arrived, his well-being was all that mattered to them. He was their world. They'd always hoped he would feel that for someone else, that the person, man or woman, would be his whole world.

Dailon had enjoyed women, but it had only been a carnal need. He loved women, but he wanted to possess a man, to savor him and leave him begging for more. He wanted to own his heart and give him the world.

And now, years later, he found himself wanting to give the world to the two men that sat across from him.

He needed to call his mothers. As seers, they probably already knew, but he had to share this happiness and this fear with someone who knew him.

Darren looked at him and then at Samuel meaningfully.

"So, what have I missed?" Dailon asked. "Please share."

Darren licked his lips and then focused on Dailon. Dailon refused to resist his need to lean over and kiss Darren softly. Before slipping his tongue in to taste more, he pulled back. Later, he would have Darren beneath him. Now was not the time.

Samuel laughed softly. "I've never known anyone else to

do this but my uncle."

"Do what?" Dailon asked. When his gaze shifted to Samuel, he realized how quiet it was around them. People were moving, breathing, but all around them, it was as if a pause button had been pressed. The people were not quite still, but very close.

Darren shook himself and glanced around. "Shit." Then he looked at Dailon with something akin to awe and fear and moved to stand.

Samuel gripped his arm. "No, Darren. It's safe. You're safe. This isn't Keith."

"But . . ." Darren shook, his gaze locked on Dailon, eyes wide with apprehension.

Dailon felt himself harden. The energy Darren sent out in waves called to him, and he found it difficult to resist. A feeling slid over him, and the need to claim Darren overwhelmed him. Inside, his darkness was stretching, reaching toward Darren.

Mine.

Dailon stood and moved to Darren, pulling him bodily out of the chair and against him, breathing him in deeply.

Keeper.

"Dailon, I've promised him he's safe with you. Don't make me question this." Samuel's voice intruded from far away.

He heard the threat in Samuel's words, but his gaze and hands were on Darren, the need overwhelming him, seeking something within.

Dailon bent and licked along Darren's neck, excited by the pulse within.

Claim me, Keeper.

"I am never a danger to him, Samuel. It is I who am in danger, my very being."

Samuel was suddenly behind him, sliding his hard body against his back. "I wondered about this, and I think Darren suspected. Let him go, Dailon. Let him go. He'll give you what you need later. Right now, let the world see us. Take deep breaths, and let's have lunch."

Samuel slid his hands up and over Dailon's waist and shoulders, then around his chest and abdomen, calming him.

Dailon bent one more time to taste Darren. His *Keeper*. A word that fought for recognition, a meaning, but Dailon couldn't find it in his head.

The darkness within recognized it, though. *Keeper*, it whispered incessantly. Dailon just wanted to drink from Darren, slice his throat with sharp teeth he didn't have, and swallow him whole.

"Dailon," Samuel warned. His touch changed until there were claws, and he grew larger, the shift obviously upon him.

Darren moaned beneath Dailon, and he breathed him in, the scent of need ripe and ready.

"Release him, Dailon," Samuel growled.

Dailon did, letting Darren fall from his hands.

Dailon took a deep breath and allowed Samuel to hold him until the feeling had passed and he was himself again.

Samuel helped him back to his chair, then bent and kissed his cheek. "There you go, Dailon. All better."

Samuel went to the other side of the table and kissed Darren's lips. "Good. Everyone's good." He pointed at the world still in slow motion around them. "Dailon."

"I don't know."

"Yes, you do. Breathe and let it happen," Samuel encouraged. "I think I would like to try the apple pie, too."

Normalcy. That was what did it, Samuel treating everything as normal. Suddenly Dailon could breathe, didn't feel like his world was falling apart, and that he had lost control of himself.

He looked at Darren, who stared back, but instead of fear, this time, there was a glint of anticipation. Dailon's world had changed. Again.

"Yes, apple pie sounds good," Darren said. "I want that, too." He glanced at him. "I want everything, but let's start with the apple pie."

Keeper, a voice whispered in the back of Dailon's mind, and he trembled.

"So," Samuel continued, "we're taking Dr. Whit's event from the classroom to the real world. We decided it will be held on pack grounds."

"We?"

Samuel smiled. "Okay, I did."

"Of course," Dailon said.

"We both know he likes challenges," Darren added.

Dailon nodded in agreement. Darren was right. Samuel did like a challenge, and perhaps the event occurring soon wasn't the only one he had in mind.

Chapter Twelve

Darren ended the call with the elder Milburn. He'd confused the partners, that was certain. Still, he was on his way to having what he'd always needed and never realized he wanted. Dailon was his Sandman. Dailon might not know it himself, but Darren felt it, especially after lunch that day. Samuel, for as much as Darren had struggled against it, was his as well.

He and Samuel had taken Dailon back to his office with only minutes to spare before Samuel had to be in class. After Samuel had taken off, Darren had rushed to his office to check into his case. Everything was progressing well on that end and required little input from him. He need only be ready to present. He was getting better at the professional side of his world.

Now he just needed to work on the preternatural side, the one that had disrupted his life. Not only had he finally admitted to himself that he was in love with Samuel, but he was also experiencing whiplash from the 360 degrees turn regarding Dailon, twisting from the fear of what he suspected Dailon was to the need to possess the man and never let him go.

He'd had no idea he would feel this way. Darren had always run away from the possibility of a Sandman in his life. Had he been told it would someday happen? Yes. Had he accepted it for himself? No. Still, he'd known. He remembered the times Aiden had pulled him aside to try and prepare him, how Danny had even tried, but he'd refused to listen. After all, his own experience with one had been a nightmare. How many nights had he found it difficult to sleep because he knew he would see Keith again in his dreams? All that changed the night he'd slept with Dailon and Samuel. It was the first time he'd been able to rest, where he felt both satisfied and safe.

He wanted that again.

Am I still afraid? Absofuckinglutely, but life is too short and too unpredictable to run from the very people who might give me happiness. The rush from playing ball, riding his bike down steep hills, or deep-sea diving was nothing compared to how Dailon had gripped him tightly. Or the way Samuel had immediately stepped in to protect them all from each other.

Darren needed that.

What confused Darren was that while he knew what Dailon was, Dailon himself appeared unaware. Of that, he was certain, given the way Dailon shook after he'd returned to his seat. The normally self-possessed man had looked around and refused to meet their eyes.

They'd talked about the plans for the upcoming event and the songs Samuel intended to play, but Dailon had remained confused and unsteady.

As for Darren, the more awkward Dailon became, the more assured Darren had felt. So much so that he had reached across the table to wrap Dailon's shaking hand in his own and squeezed gently. When he'd caught Dailon's eyes, he'd pulled him forward and kissed him softly. Samuel had slid his fingers into Dailon's hair, and the man had closed his eyes briefly.

Moments later, Dailon had returned to his commanding self, promising he would arrive at the pack grounds that week and spend time with them both. When they'd finished their meals, the three of them had returned to Dailon's building, where Samuel had stood on his tiptoes to give each a peck before heading off to class.

Dailon and Darren had watched him go, his ass lovingly

encased in those skintight pants he liked to wear. Darren knew they both wanted to see him out of those, but then Dailon slid his hand along Darren's bicep and took a deep breath.

"I know," Darren said. "I can help you with this."

Dailon nodded, and Darren pulled Dailon into his arms and held him before kissing the man again and watching him walk away as well.

Dailon was the type of man who wanted control, wanted his thumb on every iota so he could direct time the way he felt it should go.

Life has a way of throwing you a curveball or no ball at all. Then you have to figure out the next steps to take.

Darren was going to be there to make sure Dailon and Samuel took those steps with him. That was why he'd placed the call with his bosses, suggesting he remain at the Louisville office where he was needed most.

The brothers had been surprised, since Darren had begun pitching to them weeks ago how he wanted to lead the opening of the Lexington office. They'd agreed with him when he'd explained making a difference there, tackling age-old ideas that needed to be turned around. Now, Darren would make a difference in Louisville instead.

Only a few days with Samuel and Dailon, and he knew his home was wherever they were, so he'd told his bosses he wanted to stay in Louisville. They were confused with the sudden change, asking if he was certain.

Darren was. All he had to do was check his pulse when he thought about his men to know he didn't have a doubt in the world.

He suspected his relationship with Samuel and Dailon would be more than just saying they were together. If he was right, Dailon was truly unaware of who he was, what he was.

How had the man lived these many years and lacked that awareness?

When the world had stopped around them at the

restaurant, Dailon hadn't noticed it, so it had to be a natural thing for him. How many things had happened in Dailon's life he had simply accepted or even ignored? How did he handle it? What did Dailon's mothers know? Had they contributed to Dailon not knowing himself? And if they had, they had to know how dangerous it was for him to live a life this long without a Keeper.

A Coimeádaí.

Me.

I'm Dailon's Coimeádaí.

The very thought of another individual attempting to claim his and Samuel's Sandman resulted in a wave of jealousy suffusing his entire being.

No. I'll claim Dailon, and he will be ours for a lifetime to come.

First, Darren had some calls to make. He needed to speak to Danny and possibly Aiden, which only made sense, since Aiden was a Sandman. If he was going to take steps to claim a Sandman, he needed to know what such a feat would entail. Darren had no doubt they would have a great deal to say about that. How many times had they told him this day would come and he would need to be ready? Danny had worried for Darren, ever protective of him. Aiden embodied cool confidence, believing Darren could protect himself, promising he would be there to look out for him no matter what happened.

They were family. He was family. For Aiden, that meant everything, as he'd never had one. For centuries he'd known what he was, which made him believe he would live his life alone. He would either become the monster many of his kind were destined to become, or he would transition to save others. Fortunately, Aiden had found Danny before his time to choose had come.

How close was Dailon to making a similar decision?

Darren picked up the phone and dialed.

"I'm sorry. Please say that again, Darren? I don't believe we quite heard you correctly?"

Both Danny and Aiden listened closely as Darren explained that he and Samuel were together, but there was also a third.

"Now, don't get me wrong. I don't know that I'm entirely surprised, knowing our minx happens to require more than most. A threesome would seem apt, but you're saying the third may be a Sandman?" Aiden asked while two silver spheres danced above the palm of his hand.

Laidback as always, Aiden wore a pair of steel gray slacks that left nothing to the imagination, along with a loose-fitting sky-blue sweater. Marriage to Danny had settled him. The layer of intensity he'd worn in the past had eased. Aiden radiated strength and comfort now. He was still stunning to look at and turned heads wherever they traveled, but he'd lost that ever-present need to prove he was worthy to Danny's family. Not only was he loved by the man he called husband—he was also adored and respected by his mate's family.

Aiden stretched out across Darren's sofa while Danny paced back and forth. He'd interrupted Darren several times as he explained to them both what had happened over a matter of days.

"Now, this is the man that spent the night with you both?" Danny asked, pausing to look at Darren carefully.

"Yes. Aiden, I believe he's a Sandman. And yes, Danny, it's the same man. Although I never told Shelly that we slept together." *Truth is, we hardly slept that night.*

Darren laughed when Danny raised a brow. "I know it was Shelly who told you. Of course, she would know."

Danny nodded in agreement and went back to pacing again. Aiden waved a hand to set the balls on Darren's oak coffee table and reached out to pull his man into his arms.

"So, a Sandman?" Aiden said while he held Danny close,

nuzzling along his collarbone and breathing him in.

Danny and Aiden together only reinforced Darren's need to have his men close to him without questions and unknowns. He'd watched their relationship develop over time, growing comfortable together and anticipating each other's needs. They were one, rarely spending time apart, hands always reaching to touch and to hold. While it would be different for him, Dailon, and Samuel, he could see the opportunity to have something just as wonderful for himself.

Darren took a deep breath, getting himself under control. "Yes, but I don't think he knows that."

Aiden bent and inhaled his mate again before turning back to Darren. "First, we told you this day would come. Did we not, my love?"

"Yes, yes we did," Danny answered, enjoying Aiden's attention.

"And it has, you suspect," Aiden continued. "But you need some confirmation?"

"I do."

"What do you know?" Danny shifted to sit comfortably in his husband's arms.

"Not much. He was nurtured by two women, basically arrived at their doorstep."

Adrian curled one of Danny's locks around his finger and tugged.

Danny laughed. "Stop. I'm trying to focus."

"You're trying to worry, Danny," Aiden scolded. "Let's wait until we have something concrete to worry about, okay?"

Danny sighed. "So, two women. Got it. What else?"

"He doesn't go into much detail. He arrived lost and afraid. They welcomed him, created paperwork for him to attend school, and raised him as their own."

"And none of that was strange to you?" Aiden asked.

"All of it is. He just appeared, and they took him in. Even twenty years ago, someone had to notice two childless women suddenly had a twelve-year-old underfoot."

"Okay, so he's what? Thirty-two?" Danny said.

"Yes." Thirty-two with twelve years of blank history.

Aiden nodded. "I wonder if his mothers know more than they're saying. Kept his origins hidden purposefully."

"Why?"

"To keep him safe from himself and others. We arrive on this earth, expelled from the Dreamworld as if birthed. For me, I arrived hungry and desperate, afraid to trust. I was what would appear to be nine in human years. The beginning was dark, and I found myself in a system where the monsters were sometimes those who came in the guise of foster parents with sinister intentions. I was lucky to eventually find a home with a family who refused to give up on me. A doctor and his wife. It's the reason I chose this profession. But I always knew what I was, who I was."

"I don't think Dailon does."

"So, he doesn't know about the darkness. I'm surprised he's made it this long and not felt it. I struggled for years, was close to succumbing before I met my Coimeádaí, my Keeper. I knew what I needed but was too afraid to take it or even look for it."

"Had to help him realize how stupid that was." Danny turned to kiss his man. "Aiden was an ass in the beginning, but look at him now. All mine."

"Funny, must be a genetic thing . . . the asshatness?" Darren wondered.

Danny looked thoughtful. "Self-preservation, maybe? I hadn't thought of that."

"I'm in the room, babe," Aiden grumbled.

"Yes, I know, sweetheart." Danny smiled.

"But I do agree. It could be innate for us, a way to protect ourselves. We want to dominate, control, watch the world dance at our fingertips, and sink into the human psyche. Having the power to influence decisions, to see every secret revealed, is an aphrodisiac of the strongest persuasion," Aiden explained. "Still, we need balance, and this is how we end up with a human Coimeádaí. How we develop a purpose and a drive to aid rather than destroy. As a professor, he was probably guided into that service, as are most of us. And you've noticed nothing that would give another pause?"

"I've seen the control, especially with Samuel and me. He's demanding, but I think that's one of the things about him that draws us to him. I don't want to lose that."

"No," Danny glanced at Aiden. "I can promise you that won't be something you lose. It seems to be a natural characteristic for the beings."

Aiden cleared his throat, his gaze locked on Danny. "It's a two-way street. Danny is demanding and terrifyingly fierce when the moment calls for it. When I need it. He's my Keeper. Danny is the perfect balance for me, gentle when I need that and dangerous when the darkness rises. The thought is that once a Sandman has found his Coimeádaí, the darkness disappears. That's a lie."

Aiden looked back to Darren, his eyes now much darker, as if the mere mention of what waited beyond the thin veil of his humanity revealed itself. "It's always near, but I am tethered. Protected. I am safe from what lives on the other side. It's Danny's strength that feeds me."

Danny kissed Aiden gently, and the man sighed, following Danny's lips when he moved to end the touch.

"Focus. Soon," Danny whispered.

Aiden nodded and pulled Danny closer. "I can tell you that when he realizes you are who he needs, he will have some decisions to make. He will be forever changed, but it will be for the better. Life without you and Samuel would destroy him. Is that a choice you believe he'd be willing to make? Are we fated, destined to be with our Coimeádaí? Yes. But we have free will and could choose the darkness."

"Like Keith," Danny said and accepted Aiden's hand when he reached out.

"Yes, like Keith. But I would like to believe Keith was an anomaly among us. We are here to help and aid humanity, not destroy it. As with all things, the presence of so much power is intoxicating. Hence the need for our balance, for our Keeper."

"It's a great deal of responsibility," Darren said.

"It is, and you can never forget that. While Dailon's abilities could change the world, you can change him. Your love will either help him rise or, like a broken angel, make him fall and eviscerate everything he touches along the way. But it is why you are here. You and Samuel are not a random occurrence."

Darren sat down and clasped his hands. "That's what I'm thinking. We all came together, and within moments, I couldn't see any other possibility than us as one." The first time he'd heard Dailon's voice, he'd fallen for the man. Their first night together, he wanted nothing more.

He knows my heart, my fears. He knows me.

The times they'd spent together, whether eating lunch or falling asleep in a tangled mass of arms and legs, were everything Darren wanted. He didn't want to change a thing. "We have to help him see who he is."

"Yes. That's the only way you can protect each other and keep Dailon safe. I may be able to help you with that."

Darren nodded. *Whatever it takes.*

He looked up at the men before him. "Will you be at the event this weekend?"

CHAPTER THIRTEEN

Dailon lay awake and alone in his bed—no Darren, no Samuel. No one to caress and taste. It wasn't as if he had to be alone. There were any number of nubile bodies willing to host him. He only had to think it, and suddenly there would be calls and messages offering themselves as a sacrifice for his pleasure.

But that wasn't what he wanted. Those faceless strangers weren't who he needed. No, instead he thought of a beautiful brown man who matched him in height but stood with a wide frame. He pictured honey golden eyes that made him want to beg to be taken. He could all but taste the very lips he fantasized about as he gripped himself tightly, tugging his hard cock.

Darren was a delight to watch, but most importantly, Darren made him feel. Darren met him word for word, challenged him to stretch himself. Darren forced him to consider a future with someone at his side for the first time he could remember.

He makes me want to live.

And the life he envisioned wasn't just him and Darren, but the spritely Samuel as well. Samuel was a creature no man could capture without his permission. He would not be limited or forced into any mold. Samuel was pure energy, wild and free, a bit devilish, and took no prisoners. He needed a firm hand, someone not only to love him but to protect him from himself.

Dailon smiled to himself, knowing he and Darren could fill

that role. *The boy calls us his Double Ds.*

He imagined the three of them together. Darren standing behind him, his body covering him. Darren kissing him, touching him, praising him. Samuel standing in front of him, sliding fingers through his hair, caressing him, protecting him.

But from what?

Dailon found it interesting that the darkness inside him retreated from his thoughts of Darren and Samuel. Like when they'd gone to lunch, he'd heard its whispers to break and claim. The world had stopped, and he'd reached for Darren, his thoughts not his own. But Samuel had been there, brought him back from the brink, pulled him away from the edge.

So instead of breaking Darren, Dailon had wanted to beg for Darren to claim him, to wrap himself around him and keep him.

Keep me. Keep me.

The words repeated in the crevices of his mind, in his very soul. And he had no idea why.

Yet another unknown.

Dailon knew he could be hedonistic in his sexual pleasure. He didn't deny himself. He was a hunter, a taker. But here he was, willing to plead for these two men to love him.

To keep him.

Keep me. Keep me.

He ended the night restless and frustrated, unable to finish himself off, his mind too filled with unanswered questions.

The next morning, Dailon was in a car with two men he'd only known for a week. He wasn't going to count the hours he'd been in their company, because that would make what he was doing even more insane. Yet here he was, driving outside of Louisville, still confused, frustrated, and exhausted. He was on his way up into the mountains where the two women who loved him lived.

This was not the time to doubt himself.

Was it insanity to bring the men he wanted to beg to remain at his side?

Was it recklessness born of desperation?

He'd never shared his mothers with anyone before, but it felt imperative they meet.

When he'd asked the men to join him on this trip, they'd readily agreed. Samuel had no intention of going to class, because he'd had an idea the night before for a song he was writing, which he could do in the backseat of the car. Darren brought his work with him, typing away at his computer and answering calls from the passenger seat. Occasionally he would place a hand on Dailon's thigh, but then he would get back to work.

Dailon would have worried at Samuel's silence had he not heard the scratching on a fairly worn notebook he cradled in his folded legs and the mumbling.

Lots of mumbling.

"Is he always like that?" Dailon asked Darren as he turned left to take the steep climb up his mothers' trail to their home.

He often wondered how he'd made it up this hill to the front porch of their home. How had he achieved the climb and sought the shelter of two women he would love forever? And from where had he come?

Who am I?

It had been a mystery to him for years. No mother or father could he recall. As far as he knew, no one had nurtured him before the two women he'd found. Or had they found him?

"Only when he's writing. He'll be like this until he has the words written, afraid they'll leave him. I usually force him to eat once a couple of hours have passed." Darren swiped up and made a note focused on the screen.

"I'll do the same, then. Can't have our boy starve, can we?"

Darren went quiet, and even Samuel had stopped the constant mumbling that had formed the soundtrack for their travel.

Darren cleared his throat. "No, we can't allow that."

Dailon nodded and glanced over to Darren, whose eyes were utterly focused on him now. "Glad we agree. Samuel, there's a bag next to you with an apple or two. A few other snacks. Have something to eat."

A moment or two passed before Dailon heard the bag rustle and crunching blended with mumbling.

"Good boy," Dailon said and waited.

"Thank you," Samuel whispered and continued to munch.

Darren's warm fingers touched his own, and he welcomed Darren's hand. He squeezed tightly, hoping he conveyed his message.

They were in this together. Dailon and Darren would take care of Samuel, and in turn, his men would care for him.

Keep him.

Keep me. Keep me.

And this was why he'd made this drive. He'd chosen them. They were his as he hoped he was theirs.

And his mothers needed to meet the men he would work to keep in his life.

They drove a few more miles before Dailon made a sharp right, which threw Samuel, who swore loudly.

"Language, baby."

"Fuck. Fuck. Fuck. Fuck. Fuckity fuck fuck," Samuel sang. And while his voice was entrancing, such behavior would not be tolerated.

Dailon stopped the car.

"Dailon?" Darren questioned.

"A moment, Darren. A bit of correction is necessary at times." Dailon exited the car and moved to open Samuel's door.

Samuel's wide eyes, so gorgeous in their apprehension,

gave Dailon pause, but he would not begin this relationship under misconceptions. It was one thing to swear, quite another to be defiant.

Samuel locked the door, smiling at Dailon from the inside.

Then Dailon looked at Darren, who nodded and unlocked the door.

"Traitor!" Samuel shouted.

Dailon swiftly pulled the door open and tugged a struggling Samuel out of the vehicle. "No, we are a partnership, beautiful one, which means we work together to teach bratty creatures how to behave."

Dailon wasn't fooled. He could sense Samuel's eagerness, his need for curtailing, for love. Though many had allowed Samuel freedom and professed to love him, he needed a firm hand, someone who would challenge him.

Dailon dragged Samuel against him. "Singing profanities will not be tolerated when you have been warned."

Samuel tried to free himself, but Dailon's grip was tight. He grabbed Samuel's legs, lifting him until his thighs wrapped around Dailon's hips.

"Feel that, Samuel. Feel how hard you make me. I can't wait to punish you. I want to see your eyes wet with tears, but I won't do this alone. Darren?"

Darren exited the car and moved toward them.

"How many do you think?" Dailon asked.

Darren didn't fail in his response. "I believe three will serve as a reminder."

Samuel took in a sharp breath, his eyes darkened, and his tongue dipped out quickly.

"Three it is then." He nodded to Darren, then whispered to Samuel, "Deep breath, beautiful."

Darren struck.

"Darren!" Samuel's call ended in a cry of pain just before he rubbed his hard cock against Dailon's belly.

"Count, Samuel," Dailon commanded, then slid his hand over Samuel's delicious ass warmed by Darren's smack.

Samuel's face belied the excitement thrumming through him, but he shouted, "One."

"Such a good boy," Dailon praised. "Again, Darren."

The fabric of Samuel's jeans muted the slap, but Dailon felt the reverberation through to the other side.

"Count, Samuel," Darren said firmer this time.

"Two." Samuel moaned, rubbing himself against Dailon as he had before.

"Last one, baby. Darren."

The last slap was loud, and Samuel's head fell against Dailon's shoulder.

"Count, Samuel."

"Three." Samuel sniffed.

"Good boy, now we will both reward you for taking your punishment."

Dailon gently set Samuel down on the car hood, mindful of his ass. He carefully removed Samuel's jeans, eager to see how red it would be. He was not disappointed.

"Gorgeous." Dailon opened his mouth and took Samuel's leaking cock down his throat.

Samuel's cries were loud, and Dailon loved every sound. He lifted Samuel's ass and opened his thighs so Darren could lick his hole.

When they finished, a sobbing Samuel was as beautiful as a defiant one. His energy was spent, but he ate hardily. It would seem punishment worked up an appetite for their Samuel. Two problems solved rather nicely.

"You lived there?" Samuel said.

Dailon relished the awe he heard in Samuel's voice. His childhood home had to be quite the sight to take in if one had never witnessed anything like it before. Dailon's students had laughed when he told them he grew up in a treehouse, never believing the refined man before them had swung from a rope to make it to the garden house.

Dailon tried to take in the view from the eyes of someone new to his home.

Hidden high in the grouping of trees that swayed gently in the wind were seven huts. It had taken Dailon years to understand that people didn't typically sleep in trees and lacked the movement from the wind he had come to associate with safety.

Each hut had a purpose. The garden one was where Dailon had spent a lot of his time learning the uses of flowers and plants, gleaning mysteries he might apply in years to come. The library angled a few branches below, complete with a light array of seats where one could get lost for hours. A ward protected the storage hut, keeping animals away but never denied a growing young man when he was hungry.

Then there was the family hut where they all spent time together. He smiled, remembering the many nights his mothers would sing, teaching him words that seemed familiar but not, which gave him comfort and kept him safe. When he told them he thought he was gay, it had been in that space. They had both smiled and opened their arms to him. And after? They had explained how sex between two men worked. He'd asked them never to talk about that again.

Of course, they did.

Above the family space were three more huts. One for his elder mother, Cliona, another for his younger mother, Aobhill, and the third was his. While his two mothers loved each other, they'd agreed years ago to have their own space. Dailon had simply spent time in both huts until he was old enough to move to one of his own. They had never changed it, waiting for him to return home and spend time with them.

"Dailon, mine love. You have brought your loves to us at

last," Cliona called down to him. Her fiery red hair wrapped her shoulders, nearly blending into the woven shawl she wore. She curved her hand gently, and the vines extended until they reached the grassy floor. "Climb, young ones. We have waited long for you to arrive."

"Sister, they are in awe. They may need time," came Aobhill's voice from afar. She eased into view, her movements like a cat, her long white hair hanging in braids down her back.

"You with time," Cliona grumbled. "Our young one is losing time as it sifts through his fingers. Come, Darren and Samuel, Keepers of our son. With you here, we may return home."

Dailon looked to Darren and Samuel, whose gaze followed the height to where his mothers waited. He'd brought them here without explanation, driven by his own compulsion—or perhaps the women who loved him.

"Reach out to the vines. They will carry you the rest of the way." Dailon waited with a racing heart, wondering if the two men who'd taught him to breathe for the first time in years would follow him into a world of unknowns.

"That's all?" Samuel asked. "Mind if I fly instead?" And suddenly, there were wings where there shouldn't have been, iridescent and glittery like a fairy's but large enough to carry his weight. His smile as he rose was both cheeky and flirty.

Dailon loved it.

Darren didn't seem the least bit surprised. He laughed and shook his head while Samuel buffeted the air around him. Then Darren reached for the vine and allowed it to wrap around and lift him up to the ledge of Cliona's hut. Without hesitation, his mother opened her arms to Darren and hugged him tightly. She was a tall woman with strong arms that gave the best hugs when one was lost and afraid.

From the look of surprise and then joy as Darren allowed himself to be held, those arms did not disappoint.

Samuel dropped beside Darren and touched his back, but

he was more careful of hugs. Samuel was skittish like a cat, so when Aobhill leaped from her ledge down to Cliona's and landed beside him, he turned his head to regard her warily. She smiled at him in return and reached up to touch a wing gently, reverently.

Dailon allowed the vines to carry him up and stood next to his men.

"Mine son, your lover here is of our ancient blood." Cliona nodded toward Samuel. "We welcome you, child of three."

Samuel bowed kindly. "Thank you, queen over the Sidheog."

Dailon took a deep breath. "Mother?" He wondered about the recognition between one of the men he was beginning to love and the woman he'd loved as long as he'd known himself.

Am I surprised? Hasn't life always been out of the ordinary?

"Blood recognizes blood, it would seem. I welcome you as well, child of three." Aobhill opened her arms, welcoming his prickly Samuel into her embrace. "There now, we are here. Family is always near. There is nothing that happens under the sun or beneath the light of the moon without reason. Our reason has found you. Welcome."

Aobhill turned to Dailon. "There you are, son of mine. You have found your Keepers without intrusion from your overprotective mothers. You've done well, Dailon, has he not, Cliona?"

"Yes, sister. He has. Come, Keepers. Break bread with us. We bid you welcome to our hearth and home."

Chapter Fourteen

Darren was accustomed to the odd and fantastical. Having lived on Iroquois Pack land as a teenager until he went to college, he had seen some amazing things.

But this is another entire world.

What had appeared to be a network of tiny homes connected by thick vines hid expansive living quarters with space enough for several families. Why the sisters didn't share space was a question, but he wasn't there to delve into their reasons.

Now Samuel? Entirely different matter. Samuel apparently knew things about Dailon he kept to himself, and Darren was on the fence about how that made him feel.

Later, I will confront our fierce butterfly and have a few answers.

For now, he sat in a large, oversized leather chair big enough to hold not only his wide frame but perhaps his men as well. Seeing Dailon walk by once more tempted Darren to pull his pacing lover to him, but he would wait him out. Give him time.

Dailon stopped yet again and turned, one arm crossed over his broad chest and the other at his chin as he processed something. He was cute in his professor mode. All hard ass and wicked ways, but beneath the shiny exterior was a man who needed grounding.

"Dailon," Darren called to him and waited until Dailon turned, his brows raised in question. "Come sit with me, please. I'd like to hear what your mothers will share with us. Or with me, as Samuel seems not to be as blind as you and me."

"Oh, it's like a song." Aobhill laughed, delighted. "He could be a bard, Cliona."

Cliona shook her head. "My beautiful sister, it is Samuel who is the bard, the gatherer of songs. This one, Darren. He will right the wrongs."

Aobhill harrumphed. "This is why you and I cannot share a home."

Cliona laughed. "We do not share a home, my sister, because we are too different. My rainbow-colored birds of rest would drive your feline insane. It is enough that we are in the same time, even in the same place. Let us not tempt the Fates any further."

Aobhill glared before shaking her head and laughing aloud. "For truth, my sister. But anon, we shall return to our world, having seen the mates for our son."

Cliona nodded. "Yes, home. It has been many years."

"Ages," Aobhill agreed softly.

Darren barely listened to the women's chatter as he watched Samuel wander around the room, touching a book here, a tiny figurine there, clearly entranced. Darren lost what little frustration he possessed seeing the man he loved tenderly caress a vase sitting on a shelf.

"You have the carafe?" Samuel asked.

"Yes, child of three. We kept the reminder of our shared pain. It is empty of the poison I delivered to Aobhill, but its placement keeps my vision clear. And perhaps being given one from the world of dreams to care for helped ensure our feet remained steeped in the human world of reality."

"I think we did well, sister. And I forgive you. I forgave you long ago," Aobhill insisted. "We were both at fault. Not you alone."

Cliona's eyes sparkled with unshed tears. "For that, I'm grateful, but I will never forget how I let my love for someone unworthy come between us."

"Nor I, Cliona." Aobhill looked around the room. "Bread and tea? Oh, wine. This is a time for wine."

"And celebration, sister. I will retrieve the glasses."

Darren was confused, but Dailon had finally ceased his pacing and stood before him. He reached out his hand, and Dailon grasped it.

Dailon knelt, leaned in, and spoke softly. "I have never needed anyone like I need you and Samuel."

"I believe that's true. We need you as well. In days, I have changed the path I thought my life would take. I'm traveling the one for which I was destined. One with you, Dailon, and Samuel, our wondering creature. He needs us, too. Do you understand?" Darren whispered, not wanting to spook Dailon, who for the second time seemed unsure of himself.

Darren could empathize. His world had changed once. Everything he knew, lost to fear. But Danny had been there for him, and later Samuel. Always Samuel. He would be there for Dailon. They both would.

"I don't understand. Why now?" Dailon's words were soft, but he sank into Darren's arms.

Darren kissed his temple and held him close.

Cliona neared them. "There is a time for everything, my son. Now would be your time and perhaps ours. We have waited eons for you to arrive, to nurture you, and then to make sure you were safe so that our leaving would not strand you in the ocean like an unfettered broken vessel."

"Yes, and now you are safe, love, though not quite sure of your destiny, which is for you to discover." Aobhill peered at Darren. "Or perhaps you may have a little help? It would seem you have your secrets, do you not, warrior?"

Darren held Dailon close. "It's not my story to tell. I would have to agree that Dailon must discover his destiny, but I have my suspicions."

"Riddles," Dailon groaned. "I feel my entire life has been a riddle. I thought I had accepted the ignorance of my origins. I thought it was fine not remembering my life before, but I met Samuel and then Darren? My world opens up, and things I had accepted as my reality, abilities that had lain dormant, reawakened. Then I bring the men I love here, and you talk about leaving me. What does that even mean? You tell me to live my truth. What is my truth? Who am I?"

Samuel knelt beside Dailon and wet his lips with his tongue. "May I kiss you, Dailon?"

Dailon took a deep breath. "My darling. I would give you the world."

"I can have that later. But right now, a kiss would be perfect."

When Dailon bent and kissed Samuel on the lips, his entire being seemed to slip into the comfort Samuel offered. He sighed when Samuel reached up to draw him in further. Then he pulled back, his cheeks flushed and his breaths deep.

"Mmm. Your mouth is delicious, Dailon. Thank you."

Darren leaned over and kissed Samuel, too, licking the inside of his mouth. Then, satisfied, Darren sat back while Samuel spun around and settled against Dailon's side. Dailon reached forward and curled his fingers into Samuel's thick hair, grinning when Samuel leaned his head against Dailon's chest.

Cliona smiled warmly. "Your men are good for you, son." She walked away, her clothing swirling about her, returning in moments with a tray holding three teacups and a saucer of tiny biscuits. "We offer you hospitality and welcome you to our home."

Darren felt a shift in the air as he accepted a cup and a biscuit. He sensed something brush against his skin when he bit into the cookie and sipped the tea, then a feeling of welcome followed.

Cliona and Aobhill smiled. "Be welcomed."

Darren returned their smiles. "Thank you."

Cliona nodded toward Samuel but looked to Dailon and Darren, seeming to seek their permission. She smiled when they nodded, then turned to Samuel. "Child of three, we offer you hospitality and welcome you to our home."

Samuel smiled up at Darren and Dailon, who inclined their heads. He took a cup and biscuit from the tray, then tossed the biscuit into his mouth and drank the tea as well. When he remained silent, Darren cleared his throat noticeably.

Samuel bowed to Cliona and Aobhill. "Thank you."

"Of course." Lastly, Cliona offered Dailon the tea and biscuit. "Welcome home, son. We are happy to offer our home to you and to your men, our hearth to be your place of sanctuary."

"As it always has been," Aobhill added.

"And always will be," Dailon finished before he too chewed the biscuit and swallowed the tea. "Now, mothers, care to share?"

Cliona and Aobhill looked at their son and then at Darren and Samuel. The look they shared told of secrets kept. Darren braced himself.

The ride back was quiet, for which Darren was grateful. Cliona and Aobhill had watched them leave, arms wrapped around each other and waving. He had been shocked by what they had revealed and was still trying to process it all.

He broke the silence after a while. "Queen of the fairies and a princess? Your mothers? No wonder you were ready to accept our weird family."

"Please keep in mind that I knew very little about this recent discovery. Not once had my mothers alluded to being centuries old and existing during a time of fairies and banshees."

"So you never saw Aobhill become a cat," Samuel asked

while scribbling away in his notebook.

"I thought it was a pet."

"Who only appeared when your mother wasn't there?" Scribble. Scribble.

"Would you like a spanking, Samuel?" Dailon asked.

"Maybe." The smirk in Samuel's voice was too obvious.

"I promise to honor that when we arrive at my home."

"Promises. Promises." Scribble. "So the cat?"

When Aobhill had morphed into a slinky white cat before their eyes, Dailon had gone deathly pale. When they had shared their story of unfortunate love and Cliona's poisoning Aobhill because of betrayal, he and Samuel had held Dailon's hand and kept him grounded.

"It never crossed my mind."

"Or?" Samuel prompted.

Dailon sighed, "Or I couldn't fathom the truth."

"Fathom." Samuel laughed. "He said fathom."

"Miscreant."

Samuel laughed again. "Your miscreant. Well, yours and Darren's, of course. So now what?"

Dailon sighed. "Now, I accept that my mothers were never human as I'd thought. I have always known I was different than humans, but what am I?"

"I have an idea," Darren said. "I'm sure Samuel does, too. But we both want you to speak with Samuel's Uncle Aiden first to be sure."

"More secrets," Dailon growled.

"I'm sorry, but yes. We need to be sure before we throw you another curve. Aiden will know."

"And he'll be at the concert this weekend," Samuel added.

"He will?"

"Yes, I asked him," Darren replied. "Both he and Danny have agreed to be there for the evening. Since it's on pack grounds, they won't have to have their security team and can relax for a change."

"Security team?" Dailon asked.

"Yes. Danny is the alpha's son . . . his human son. Jeremiah is very protective where Danny is concerned. He never travels alone anymore."

Dailon nodded. "So he and this Aiden will be there, and just by meeting me, Aiden will be able to determine what?"

Darren winced. "That you are who Samuel and I suspect you are. That's all you're getting for now. Keep your eyes on the road."

Dailon grinned, and suddenly time slowed until they were the only ones moving at an average pace. Other cars on the road advanced in slow motion.

"You're doing it again, Dailon," Darren said.

"You said for me to keep my eyes on the road. I can feel the other drivers. I can help them drift." There was a different voice there beneath the surface, inhuman. "I can make them stop. Every. Single. One."

"Dailon?" Darren spoke softly to soothe Dailon.

"Keeper?" Dailon whispered.

"Yes, Dailon. I'm your Keeper. We both are. Samuel?"

"I'm here." Samuel leaned against the front seat. "One little sip."

"Little, yes," Darren agreed. "Any more would be too like a claiming, and we're not ready."

Samuel nodded and then was at Dailon's throat, fangs deep.

"Let me go," Dailon growled.

"No, Dailon. You will let the people go, and then we're going to go to your home." Darren reached over to rub Dailon's thigh as Samuel drank. "Deep breaths, baby. There you go. Much better."

Dailon's grip on the wheel tightened as he fought the creature within.

"Pull to the side, Dailon," Darren ordered. "I'm going to drive. You're going to sit in the back with Samuel, who will keep an eye on you."

At his name, Samuel rose, licking Dailon's blood away from his lips.

"Samuel?" Dailon whispered, his voice scratchy.

"I have you, Dailon. Pull over like Darren said. You need to rest. Let me help you."

Darren hoped they would be able to make it to the weekend. If not, he and Samuel might just have to claim their Sandman.

Chapter Fifteen

Samuel waited at the corner outside his afternoon class. Both his men had insisted on picking him up, no longer satisfied with pack members driving him to and from pack lands.

For his part, Dailon had decided Samuel needed a car, claiming he had to be trusted to be the adult he was. His only limits should be those Dailon and Darren gave him. And of course himself. On the other hand, Darren worried about trusting him at the helm of a moving hunk of metal.

Today would be the first of his lessons, and while he was excited, he could also admit to being a tad nervous.

He looked at his phone and smiled at the last string of messages between Darren and him.

There's still time to change your mind.

Don't want to. Dailon trusts me. Why can't you?

The thought of you driving makes my heart race.

You can't always be there, Darren. Dailon's right. If I'm going to be respected by my family, taking charge of my transportation is the first step.

I know, but I don't have to like it. Okay, give us about ten minutes. We had to pick up a few things.

Okay.

Dailon said to get off the phone and stop worrying.

Tell him he's right, and thank you. Now, get your asses here so I can learn how to drive.

Showing this one to Dailon. You know how he likes to remind you of your manners.

Samuel laughed, put away the phone, and adjusted his

hard dick in his skintight jeans. There was no way anyone could miss his response to Darren's promise, and he found himself not caring. He had two guys who checked to see if he ate, who called him in the morning, contacted him throughout the day, and met him after class to take him home. He basked in Darren's overprotectiveness and Dailon's corrections. They loved him the way he had always wanted.

"So you're fucking both of them, huh," an irritating voice huffed from behind him.

Samuel recognized the voice. "Oh, hey, Dick."

"Richard."

"Same thing."

"No, you're the dick."

Samuel scrutinized Richard. If he were interested in beautiful boys who looked like they enjoyed swimming and riding horses, Richard might do it for him. But no. Darren and Dailon made him feel safe and cared for. Yeah, there might be a few hiccups along the way when the ancient being crawling around in Dailon's psyche appeared, but he knew of no one he would rather have by his side than Darren and Dailon. His Double D's. His rocks.

Richard? Fuckable and forgettable.

"Richard, Dick, whatever your name is, I don't have time for this. What do you even want? We never talk beyond our group meetings, and suddenly you feel the need to share the air I breathe? A little distance, please."

"Do you always have to be an ass?"

"Not always and not with everyone. You warrant my special care." Samuel raised a brow before focusing on the road again.

His phone dinged, and he realized he'd forgotten to respond to Cam's message. Both Cam and Filly would be there tomorrow, and Samuel needed to make arrangements to meet them at the airport. It was too soon to think he would be able to pick them up by himself, but perhaps if he were good, he would be allowed to drive them to their hotel. It was a thought.

Samuel had been taking a break from music to go to school, get a degree. He'd thought his bandmates would appreciate the holiday as well, but they'd both insisted they were bored. The moment he'd mentioned a concert with a small gathering but a considerable cause, they were all in immediately making arrangements to visit. A word or two to their pack in California, and they were on their way. Filly and Cam were wolves who had looked beyond Samuel's hybrid blood and straight to the heart of the fellow musician within. They didn't take Samuel's shit, which he loved. They understood each other and got along well, and they'd never fucked, which made things perfect. Crossing that line had never come to mind. They made music, not conflict. Sure, they fought. What bands didn't? The music they made was always more important, music was what mattered to all of them, so they cast the petty shit aside.

After their talk the previous week, each had claimed he was different. Filly had *heard something* in Samuel's voice and suddenly three-wayed Cam into the call. They'd made plans, but Samuel was pretty confident one of their goals was to discover the reason why he sounded so happy or different.

He could have told them it was his Double Ds, but he was still a little afraid to say it out loud.

Samuel had dreamed of being loved completely and absolutely for so long. Then to find what could honestly be his happy ever after in not just Darren but Dailon as well? Heaven. The only hiccup? Dailon didn't know he was a Sandman. Dailon's inability to identify that part of himself gave Darren and Samuel cause to worry. They were his Keepers, though. They were meant to be.

It hadn't taken much to recognize Cliona and Aobhill, the

queen and her sister. They'd made him promise to allow Dailon to discover himself. Bound by the ties of the world he lived in—thanks to his mother and father—he heeded the lessons taught to him. His parents had deemed it paramount for him to learn the expectations of the world in which he lived. Rules of the Glen. The muck of the muck.

Child of Three: his mother, his father, and the Glen. He carried three forms. He was a hybrid and would always be, but he remained a member of the Seelie-Unseelie world. The Glen. He knew the tongue and the customs.

He had been asked to keep his mouth shut, and he would.

He glanced to his side only to realize Richard the Dick was still standing there.

"Look, I know I can be a jerk," Richard grumbled.

Samuel wasn't going to argue with that. It was like the man hated him, and he had no idea why. He had tried at first to be friendly because, believe it or not, he liked people. Sure, he gave them a hard time, but he enjoyed helping others, and he could be a good friend. Okay, so he forgot a few details, and keeping himself restrained or even focused was sometimes an impossible task. But he liked to think he was better than Richard had given him the chance to be. There were only so many rebuttals he could take before he couldn't resist playing with the silly human.

A puddle of water magically appearing here.

A sudden breeze causing a missed step there.

Then Samuel would offer to help only to be snarled at irritably.

So, Samuel had said *what-the-fuck-ever* and stopped trying.

He could almost hear Dailon in the back of his brain whispering *be good*. He shivered with thoughts of being pleasured long into the morning hours if he was, in fact, good.

But a man could only take so much, and Richard had reached the limit.

"Then why the hell are you, Richard? What do you want?" Samuel spun around and waited.

Richard looked at him as though struggling to say something, but no words came out.

"Fine. Just remember to be there tomorrow at seven." Samuel glared. "The band will do five songs, although knowing Filly and Cam, it could be more than that."

A horn blared, and Samuel heard his name called sharply. His men had arrived. Nothing else mattered.

Samuel left Richard standing there and almost flew to the car before he quickly caught himself.

Landing in the back, he reached forward to kiss first Dailon, then Darren.

"What was that about?" Darren asked.

"I don't know. Don't worry about it."

"We have to worry, Samuel," Dailon added. "We still don't know who shot at my car or if you're in danger."

"We haven't heard anything. I don't want to think about that. Let's go practice driving, and maybe I can be the one to drive when we get the guys?"

Darren coughed.

Dailon laughed. "Our eager boy, Darren, wants to prove himself."

"He wouldn't be Samuel if he didn't try."

"Oh, shut up, and let's go."

Samuel smiled at his bandmates as they exited the gate at the airport. Filly and Cam would have fit perfectly on the cover of a GQ magazine. Filly, with his shoulder-length black hair, baby blue shirt, and dark jeans, walked over to him and hugged him tightly. Cam, built slim and athletic, wore his hair braided past his shoulders. But the black skintight leather skirt he wore with the nearly six-inch heels was bound to throw off most onlookers, while others might appreciate the view.

"Come here and give me a kiss, beautiful," Cam sang, and heads turned.

Samuel didn't hesitate, leaning out of Filly's tight hug to plant a soft kiss on Cam's lips. When his tongue dipped in, he groaned then shouted at the pinch on his hips. "Ouch."

"Settle down and allow me to meet your bandmates," Dailon ordered. "And the only mouth I want you sampling is mine or Darren's, Samuel. So you'd do well to remember that."

"Oh, Samuel, you got yourself a Daddy?" Cam's smile was pure evil. "It's about time someone reined you in. So now, Samuel's Daddy, please don't worry about me. I'm not a threat. Just friends." Cam blew Dailon a kiss. "Hi, Darren."

"Hi, troublemaker. Come hug me."

"Of course," Cam said and giggled when Darren picked him up for the hug. "So many muscles." He squeezed Darren's arms and stepped back. "So, a little bird told us Samuel has two Daddies now, his Double Ds?"

Darren nodded. "Yes, we're his."

Dailon followed with, "And he's ours."

Cam raised an arched brow and smiled. "Good to hear. Finally. So, Filly and I are ready for a real meal. Let's go."

"I'm driving," Samuel shouted.

Darren put the kibosh on that immediately. "Nope. Can't take another ride like that one right now. I'm driving, and you're sitting in the back to chat with Filly and Cam."

Samuel pouted. Cam's laugh was not welcome, not welcome at all.

Samuel, Filly, and Cam played late into the night. Samuel had two new songs he wanted to try out, something different. He sang a few words and explained what he heard as accompaniment. When Filly strummed along and Cam picked up with the drums, it was perfect.

They were in Samuel's studio, a room in his basement he'd set up strictly for music. Dailon and Darren were upstairs talking, but Samuel hadn't missed the looks Dailon had been sending Darren's way. Dailon wanted Darren, needed him.

When he had to start over . . . again . . . Cam and Filly shook their heads.

Filly raised his hand. "Let's take a break. You can't focus, and we're tired. Gotta say, though, love looks good on you. Have your men heard your songs?"

"No, it's a surprise." He hadn't shared a word with them. When they heard them, it would be the first time. He needed it to be perfect.

Cam nodded. "Well, I think they're both beautiful."

"My men?"

"Your men are gorgeous, babe, but I was talking about the songs. Now, what's this about someone trying to shoot you?"

Samuel shrugged. "There's nothing to worry about."

"It has to be something if your guys are talking about it now. Something about you arguing with a guy from your study group."

Of course Cam's wolf ears would hear Dailon and Darren talking no matter how quiet they were trying to be. So Samuel filled his bandmates, his friends, in on what happened.

"Well now, Samuel. That does have me a bit worried about you," Cam growled. "Even if I can heal from one, a bullet hurts, and I'd rather you not be hurt."

Most people would look at the three of them and assume Cam was a delicate thing because he was the softer looking of them. Cam was dangerous and bloody, ready to eviscerate any creature posing a threat to someone he loved. No, it was Filly, solid and massive, arms bigger than Samuel's thighs, biceps like melons, with legs that went on forever, who was the softy. He also had the sweetest soul, and his compassion for others was vast.

The concerned look on Filly's face made Samuel reach out to him, touching his wrist gently. "I'm fine, Filly. Promise."

"You know, Cam and I were planning to head back home Sunday evening, but we can stay if you need us, can't we, Cam?"

Cam smiled gently and nodded. "Of course, Filly."

"No, there's no need to do that," Samuel responded.

Darren entered the room with Dailon. "Samuel's right. You can go home. The pack hasn't ceased keeping an eye out, whether Samuel wants them to or not. I'm here, and so is Dailon."

"But I thought you were working in another city." Cam raised a brow in question.

Darren cleared his throat. "Things changed."

"What things?" Samuel asked. "Darren, what did you do?"

"I worked it out to remain at the Louisville office and switched places with Todd for the Tennessee office."

Dailon huffed. "I take it this is new information for you as well, Samuel?"

"Yes, it is. I would love to know what made you go back on a decision you were so proud of weeks ago. I'm fine. Yes, I admit I was having a bit of a tantrum."

"Bit?" Dailon repeated.

Samuel might have felt embarrassed, but he would ignore that for now. "Yes, bit. Things are different now."

"Well, that's just it, Samuel. Things aren't just different for you. They're different for all of us," Darren said. "And right now, I want my focus to be on us. I can always head up a new office or move away as long as you are there with me. You and Dailon. I want to be here with you both, so I made changes."

Samuel nodded, but he was still upset that Darren had given up his dream.

"Baby?" Darren asked.

"So, Cam and I are going to step out, maybe go upstairs and watch television with the volume up loud," Filly said while gently pushing Cam in front of him.

"We are?" Cam asked.

"Yes, Cam, we are."

"But this is so much more interesting. Daytime TV drama and everything."

"Cam!"

"Fine. Fine. I need to polish my nails anyway."

"That's the spirit."

Chapter Sixteen

Darren had good intentions. He did. The time they'd spent together the last few weeks was a roller coaster of moments. They met with the family to report on Samuel's safety. The three of them were nurturing their relationship. No, there hadn't been the perfect moment to tell the men in his life that he'd changed directions, that while they'd been thinking of how they could make a long-distance relationship work for the three of them, Darren had put a plan in action for them to simply be together.

He'd been settling into his new office, essentially a more spacious one than the one he had. He had an assistant and the promise of a hefty sum for the future. He was fine. No, he wasn't starting a new adventure someplace else. Instead, he was beginning his life with the two men he loved. That was what mattered—nothing else.

"I was going to tell you." He glanced at Samuel and Dailon, trying to judge their reactions.

"When?" Samuel asked, so beautiful in his fiercely overprotective stance. "Opening a new office in Tennessee was all you talked about for months. The changes you were going to make. The connections. The location. That's all I heard about. I was preparing myself for when you had fully moved there, and I would have to get used to life without you. Then this." He flipped his hand around like a dying fish indicating Darren and Dailon.

"Now you don't have to. I'm right here, and I'm not going anywhere."

"But why?" The question filled with anguish and confusion.

Darren wanted to draw Samuel into his arms, but they needed to talk. Holding Samuel right now would only distract him, and Samuel and Dailon wished to understand his reasons.

"Come here, baby." Dailon held out his arms.

There was no hesitation. Samuel went, and Dailon held him close, his chest against Samuel's back, his arms wrapped in front of him, so Samuel could listen and not run. It was one thing to tease, to joke around, to make love, but it was quite another to be honest about their feelings for one another. Being vulnerable was new to all of them, a different dynamic. They were no longer dancing around what could be. They were well past that.

It was scary because who knew what would happen down the road, but Darren would control what he could and ride along for the rest. He was determined to live with the two men he loved.

Darren had no doubt Samuel loved him. And he knew he and Samuel weren't alone in this and not the only ones afraid. He glanced at Dailon, whose expression held such longing it made his heart stutter.

Darren had everything to lose here, and he refused to let that happen. "Because I now have two people I want in my life forever. Because you both matter to me. Because I don't want to be apart. While Tennessee is only hours away, it's the *away* part I don't care for when I only want to be next to you. I want to wake up in bed with you, sit at Dailon's breakfast table, listen to you mumble lyrics for your next song, and know that I'm in the right place. Home. I want my home. You and Dailon are my home."

Tears tracked over Samuel's cheeks, and while Darren was sorry he'd been the one to cause them, he refused to take one word back. He wouldn't apologize for finally taking what was rightfully his. Samuel and Dailon were his.

He made sure both Dailon and Samuel heard him when he spoke. "You're my forever."

Samuel's eyes shifted, the depths black, the pupils blown. "You're my forever. Our forever." He looked up at Dailon.

Dailon nodded. "Forever. When Dr. Marshall told me about you, Samuel, I had no idea that you would lead me to realize a broken dream I've always had. Perhaps it was one I hid from myself, the thought that I could be loved, could be kept. I want to be kept by you both. I don't know why those words mean so much, why they make me tremble inside when nothing has ever made me afraid before. But I need you to keep me. Do you understand? Do you both understand? I don't even understand why."

Dailon trailed off, and Samuel turned to him, sheltering him and kissing him, holding off the change they could all feel at the surface.

Darren joined them, his arms wide enough and strong enough to encompass them together. "We understand, Dailon, and we promise to keep you. We have you."

Dailon shuddered, his emotional whirlwind ripping at Darren. He wanted to tell Dailon the truth, but Dailon had to be the one to figure it out. He had to be the one to ask to be claimed. To do that, Dailon had to learn who he was.

When Dailon turned to him, his mouth seeking, Darren obliged him with a deep kiss. Then he moaned when he felt fine slim fingers reach into his pants and wrap around his cock. Samuel. Strong hands pulled his pants down, followed by the thump of knees on the carpeted floor. A wet mouth surrounded his cock, a tongue doing beautiful things to his body.

"Samuel," Darren groaned.

"Yes, that's my name. Open Dailon's pants. I want both of

your dicks in my mouth right now. I want to swallow your cum."

"Now?" Darren asked.

"Yes, right the fuck now."

"Language," Dailon managed in a quaky voice.

"Yeah, okay, language, Dailon. You can spank my ass later. Right now, let me taste you."

Dailon smiled softly and moved back to allow Darren to unbuckle his slacks. His face was still flush as evidence of his earlier turmoil, but his eyes were bright with need.

"Yeah, you need this. We all do," Darren said. "Good job, Samuel. Open your mouth wider. Good. Let me feel your teeth. That's it."

Darren rocked in and out of Samuel's throat while he tugged Dailon's dick from his pants. The sight of Dailon's pre-come tempted him to have a taste of his own.

But Samuel was doing this for them all, so he helped feed Dailon's dick inside Samuel's obscenely wide mouth. He nearly came from the wet suction and slip-slide of Dailon's dick beside his in Samuel's mouth.

Together, he and Dailon alternately fucked Samuel's throat, kissing each other and taking turns to slide in deep while the other slid out.

The slippery wet sound Samuel made was enough and too much.

One more shove and Darren was coming, and as if his pulse of seed was the trigger, Dailon exploded, his head back and his voice a roar of release.

It was magnificent.

It was also quite the attention-getter.

"Wow," Cam hollered downstairs. "That had to be amazing. Peeksie?"

Samuel, still licking their cocks, shouted back. "No, bitch."

That night they decided to go to Emerald Fawn, a Japanese steakhouse Dailon loved. The five of them chatted and laughed while enjoying trays of sushi and steak, seaweed salad, and teriyaki chicken.

Samuel sat between him and Dailon. If he wasn't touching Samuel, Dailon was. For the first time in years, Samuel wasn't putting on some type of show. Instead, he was relaxed, settled against his chair, spending time with his friends.

Dailon spent time observing them all, but his hand would slide along Samuel's thigh, or he would draw a finger along Darren's shoulder. Eventually, he settled in and got to know the crazy band members.

It was pleasant, and Darren was happy with his decision to enjoy this gift.

"Darren, I always said Samuel should just drug you and drag you off. You know like . . . What was that movie?" Cam asked no one in particular.

"Misery," Dailon said.

"Yes. But not with the breaking ankles bit. This right here?" Cam pointed at the three of them with a swirl of his fingers. "This was meant to be. Even though there's something off about you, Dailon, no offense, I know you're the right one for our guy. It almost makes me want to drug someone and do a little kidnapping myself. What do you think about that, Filly?"

Filly's eyes widened.

"Want me to kidnap you and ride your dick or make you ride mine," Cam continued. "I mean, while people are figuring things out and all, think you could get a clue or two?"

Filly choked, and the beer he was drinking flew from his fingers. It would have hit Samuel, but Dailon raised his hand, pausing it mid-launch, spun it about with a flick of his fingers. Everyone watched as it landed back in front of Filly, who was still taking great gasping gulps of air.

Cam looked at Dailon thoughtfully, sliding a purple nail across his chin. "Now, isn't that interesting? Care to share, Dailon? It would seem there are a few unknowns we may need to address." There was a dangerous glint to his eyes.

Darren had been around wolves enough to know when one was close to the surface. Cam's eyes slid from green to gold, his features sharpening. Filly stopped choking and flanked Cam, who was still human but completely alert.

"I wish I could tell you. I would if I knew myself. I can say that my lovers seem to know another part of me. Even my mothers apparently know. Yet none will tell me. I am on some type of quest, one to discover who I am. What I do know is that these men are keeping me safe and perhaps those around me safe as well."

Cam turned his gaze to Samuel.

"I'm not worried, Cameron," Samuel said. "You shouldn't be either."

Cam's stare was intense. "The unknowns don't concern you?"

Samuel smiled. "No. No, they don't." His expression was warm when he took Cam in. "Still, it's lovely knowing you are ready to kick ass if I need you."

Cam looked Dailon up and down. "Always." A quick nod, and he reached out to touch Filly's back.

Filly settled, picking up his beer and taking a drink. He sighed when Cam slid his hand up his back and across his shoulder. The two always enjoyed touch, particularly with each other, but Darren had no idea if they were in a relationship. It wasn't as if wolves weren't a tactile group, taking comfort in proximity. It was one of the things Darren adored about Samuel, his need for touch.

"What I do know is I have found my place with Samuel and Darren," Dailon continued. "For the first time, I have someone for me other than the women who raised me. While they kept secrets from me, I still trust them. My mothers see something in these two that makes them happy, gives them the strength to return home to a place they left eons ago."

Darren reached for Dailon's hand then, and his lover held on tight. Dailon's mothers had only been waiting for Dailon to be safe before moving on to live their lives. And apparently, to them, that safety was with Darren and Samuel. Mysterious women, but there was no doubt they loved their son.

"They would leave you alone here," Filly asked, his voice sounding sad.

"Dailon will never be alone," Samuel said. "We will be here for him." Samuel looked at Darren. "Both of us."

Darren couldn't resist bending down to kiss him.

"Awww," Cam sang. "As long as you're happy, Samuel, we're happy."

"Thank you, Cam," Samuel said, the earlier tension dissipating. "We are."

Chapter Seventeen

The gardens were beautiful. Samuel had no idea who Kristoff had hired to decorate for the event, and if he was honest, he didn't care. He trusted Kristoff to make sure whoever he hired would benefit from being tied to the pack and support others. Helping the community was paramount to Kristoff. He never went for the big name or the award winners. He chose people who needed help and would give the best work.

And they had. The whole garden seemed to glow with lanterns sprinkled strategically. Grandmother Sarai, his grandfather's first mate, had designed the garden. There were roses both climbing and wild. Bushes of the fragrant flowers followed a path through the gardens and up to where Samuel, Cam, and Filly would perform.

There were chairs spaced about the garden floor, and already ushers escorted guests to their seats while Samuel stood hand in hand with Darren and Dailon, his Double Ds.

Dailon looked magnificent in his tailored suit. His shirt opened at the neck, revealing skin mottled with marks both Samuel and Darren had placed there the night before.

Samuel stood between his guys, butterflies in his stomach. He was nervous, but it wasn't because of the audience or even the grade for his class.

"Samuel, are you okay?" Darren asked.

As long as they'd known each other, it had always been easy for Darren to sense his worry. His protector and his best friend. He couldn't resist the smile at that thought, the warmth in his belly right next to those butterfly wings.

Dailon turned to him. "Samuel?"

"It's okay, guys, I promise. Just excited. Big or small, there are people here who will hear the music from my heart and soul."

"Well, they will love it, and if they don't, they aren't worthy. But, from the glances we keep getting, I would say they are very interested in your heart and soul." Dailon picked up his hand and nipped playfully at his wrist.

Samuel's butterflies fluttered for an entirely different reason then. "Stop before you draw blood."

"We haven't moved there yet, but I would love to taste your blood whenever you're ready for me to experience it."

Samuel's dick hardened at the thought. He could sense they were getting closer to the claiming, but he had no idea if Dailon was even aware of what he needed.

Samuel would have to trust Darren to watch their Sandman while he performed later. Too many times, Dailon's dark creature within had surfaced.

Darren responded to Dailon's comment. "Whenever you are ready to be fed, Dailon, both Samuel and I will care for your needs."

Dailon nodded and turned to look over the crowd, the seats filling rapidly. He seemed out of sorts, like he was on edge or something. Was it his need to be claimed? Samuel and Darren would take care of that as soon as Dailon knew for himself what he was and could say he was ready.

Dailon seemed to thrum with an energy Samuel could feel in his bones. It was hard to focus on the stage or the audience preparing to listen to them play when that energy was calling to him, begging him to taste and touch. Samuel sexed him up with his eyes, trying to determine where the three of them could have a little privacy.

"Who is that?" Dailon asked as he stared with wonder . . .

And recognition?

He followed Dailon's gaze to see Danny and Aiden walking toward them. Aiden wore a body-fitting virgin wool serge suit, his long black hair pulled into a queue. Danny's plum-colored suit complemented Aiden's cobalt blue one. Danny's hair was in a twisted updo with tendrils falling into his face, the ends reddened from the sun.

"My uncles Danny and Aiden," Samuel acknowledged.

"I need to meet him."

He knew which man Dailon felt compelled to meet. The energy thrumming from Dailon increased to a near hum reverberating over his skin the closer Aiden came. Like attracted like, it would seem. Brother recognizing brother.

"Aiden, he's the one with the eyes glowing, very much like your own," Darren observed.

Samuel looked at Dailon to see that Darren was right. Dailon's eyes had slid from their usual blue to a blending of silvery mercury and blue that danced.

"Which is the one in the dark blue suit? I feel . . . I am overwhelmed by feeling." Wonder swirled in Dailon's curiously transitioning eyes.

Samuel reached for him. "Aiden. His name is Aiden."

"Aiden," Dailon repeated. "I know him."

"I thought you might. Let's introduce you."

When Aiden stood before him, he opened his arms. "Brother."

Dailon's cry was a sob, filled with pain and hope and joy. "Brother. My brother."

Darren smirked. "It looks like they took care of that for you, Samuel."

"Yeah, baby. They did."

Samuel held onto Darren's hand as they watched Dailon cry into Aiden's shoulder. Aiden slid his hand over Dailon's back, speaking too soft for even a wolf to hear.

And then they were gone.

Dailon held tight to Aiden, relief at being found overwhelming him. He had no idea what connected him to this man, but he knew they were a part of each other. They were brothers.

"Lift your head and look around, Dailon."

Dailon took a deep breath and raised his head. He saw nothing.

"Look deeper. Listen and hear from within."

Dailon shuddered. Here he was, stronger than most, one who dictated to others. In the last few weeks, his life had changed so much. He didn't even know Aiden, not really, but his voice compelled him to listen.

He knows who I am.

Words. Thoughts. Images. They all began to form and build, layer upon layer, until the space about them became filled with depth and range.

"Touch," Aiden said. "Don't change, though. Just reach forward, breathe, and touch."

Dailon looked at Aiden, and Aiden urged him to step forward. Dailon reached out and grasped a thought, and before he could take that breath, he flew.

I'm always the one in the background doing all the work while he gets front stage. Even his home. What the fuck is this? Who knew he lived like this?

It was one of the people at the event. Dailon could hear his thoughts. Or her thoughts? It felt like a man. Wait. He could feel the person's emotions.

I told him where to park. He better fucking remember.

"Not only can you feel them, but you can change them. And that is one of the reasons why we need a Keeper, someone who will make sure what we do will not cause harm. We choose to help until the darkness within us chooses to control."

The first person was jealous of Samuel, of his Keeper. Dailon could feel that. Change. He could change that, could give him a different thought.

He took a deep breath and spoke, "You will respect Samuel; see him as I see him."

"No, Dailon. Don't. Think. Would you want that, someone to see Samuel as you do? What you have with Samuel and Darren is sacred. If you aren't careful with your words, with what you speak into their dreams, it can become twisted."

There was a shift, this time, anger and grief.

I could love him, show him that I'm worth his time. He doesn't see me. I could make him see me.

Need. The need was overwhelming.

"Dailon, breathe and release. I will restore us. I only wanted you to experience this, to see what you are."

Dailon flew back, or at least his spirit did, but a part of him wanted to stay, to shred, to twist the mind that threatened his Keeper. *Destroy.*

Then calm pervaded his mind, wrapped around him. The voices of his men calling to him, soothing him until the frustration was no longer.

Dailon looked around, testing, then sifted once again through the crowd. Excitement, curiosity, and pleasure. A need to help existed among many while others were nervous about grades and impressing Dr. Marshall.

This was much more than he'd ever experienced before. *I can hear them all. Feel them all. It's surreal. Is this another plane, a different world?*

"Where am I?" Dailon asked.

Aiden stood before him again, skin glowing with power, eyes vivid as they blended from one color into another with a lava light effect.

Aiden waved a hand, indicating all around them. "This is a part of the Dreamworld. It's a sliver of reality you, me, and our brothers share, where we weave the dream. It's where humans and even some others dream. We can hear them. We can change them. We can direct their thoughts."

Sandman. I'm a Sandman.

Dailon had heard the stories, had listened to his mothers read them as a child.

All this time, they were trying to help me discover my identity.

He remembered the tales now, the stories of power and control, of the ability to step into another's dreams, to enter their fantasies and change them.

Dailon listened to the thoughts and wishes of those in this Dreamworld. He heard their fears and their prayers.

He thought back to his reaction the day he and his men had gone to the zoo. He was not a fan of crowds, had always found them overwhelming. There was an odd pressure in groups of people that pushed against his mind, pulled at him, and awakened his inner darkness. He'd felt it that day, and the more agitated he became, the more those around him sought to be closer, moving toward him. A touch from Samuel and Darren had eased the pressure so he could breathe.

Even now, he felt Samuel and Darren nearby, knew they were giving him time to do this, to experience this with the safety of someone who fully knew himself.

A brother.

Aiden.

"I am a Sandman."

"Yes, brother. You are, and though I can feel the darkness within you, I'm not worried. You don't carry the taint of one poisoned against humanity. So accept the claiming of your mates, your Coimeádaithe. You can wield the darkness rather than be wielded."

"Coimeádaithe."

"Your mates. My nephew Samuel and Darren are your Coimeádaithe as Daniel is mine. Years ago, Daniel came into my hospital severely beaten through abuse, and I treated him. We had a shaky start, he and I. We hated each other at first.

But I could feel something about him. I recognized his power over me, the potential to be what I had needed for hundreds of years but feared I didn't deserve.

"Daniel had been entangled with Keith, one of our brothers too deep in his twisted darkness to recognize Daniel's light for what it was. Instead, he used Daniel, drank in his energy, refusing to be claimed." Aiden paused for a moment

When Dailon said nothing, Aiden continued. "When Daniel had finally escaped, Keith came after him and eventually me, and because of us, Darren."

It explained a great deal, the reason Dailon had originally seen fear in Darren's eyes before the trust, the tenderness. There were shadows of a past in which he'd had no part, but he played such an immense role.

"You blame yourself?" Dailon asked.

"I did, for years. Had I not accepted Danny's place in my life, perhaps Darren would not have been harmed. He wouldn't have been so afraid to love, but his past and fears helped him attain his future. Right now, he's able to provide solace for others, to champion for change."

"To enjoy the good, you must sometimes overcome pain." Dailon nodded

"While this is true, I would not have wished that for him. Still, we are all closer. We are family, and after being alone for years, I would destroy anything and anyone who endangered it."

Dailon didn't miss the veiled threat. He understood Aiden's need to protect Samuel and Darren. He felt the same way, even more so, because he loved them both. "I would protect them with my life."

Aiden nodded, his eyes glinting suddenly. "Our time grows short here. Samuel summons me. He wants his man back." He smiled.

Dailon chuckled. "He can be impatient, my little one."

"Yes, he has never seen the need to wait. Even now, I feel his thoughts pressing against me for you to return. I will leave you with this. There is a claiming that must occur to seal the bond between the three of you. I will assume it works the same way as it does when there are two."

"A claiming?" Dailon shivered, remembering his mothers' tales.

"Yes, a submission, blood rights. It is the way with us to have our Coimeádaí mate us, possess us," Aiden stated. "Have you seen yourself, Dailon? Seen what you can become?"

Dailon startled when the air about them shimmered, and suddenly Aiden was no longer human. He was massive, his arms extending past his knees, hands ending in vicious talons. He twisted his monstrous head back and forth, rocking it and stretching his long neck.

"It's been a while since I've shifted fully." Aiden spread his arms, stretching out his body. "I don't visit the Dreamworld in my entire form as often as I should. I don't have the time, but sometimes my mate will ask me, will want to claim me here as well." He licked his wide lips, his fork tongue sliding over his maw of sharp teeth.

Aiden's yellow eyes tracked him. "This is what I can become, what you can become. The worst of nightmares dragging others toward their fears and manipulating their futures. But then I am also this . . ."

There was an explosive wave and the brightest of lights. It was all Dailon could see.

"The light to my darkness, what my claiming has helped me to become." Aiden's voice emanated from the light. "There are two sides to us, one of immense darkness and the other of light. Our Coimeádaí knows and possesses both. They protect us and keep us. They treasure us and help us to harness what could quickly become destruction. They are our safe place."

"Samuel and Darren," Dailon murmured.

"Yes." The light dissipated, replaced by Aiden's human form. "Samuel and Darren, who have been waiting patiently to take you."

"They knew." Dailon suddenly realized that this was what his men hadn't been able to tell him.

"Yes. And even though Darren was afraid, his need for you eclipsed his apprehension of what you could become. He remembers Keith, can never truly forget, but he has gained patience with you and sought me out, knowing what you were. He and Samuel both have you at the forefront of their thoughts. And probably unknowingly, each had come to me to determine how best to help their lost Sandman." Aiden's smile was warm. "Samuel has never cared for anyone other than Darren. He has always been a powerful brat who loved to play, to the detriment and frustration of many. You have helped him to grow, to reach. He needs you. They both do. And you need them."

"I do. I need them both," Dailon agreed.

The light around Aiden grew brighter again, and Dailon knew he'd pleased the man. "Am I like you?"

"Like me?"

Dailon pointed to himself. "I've never seen myself in any other form than human. The man you see before you."

He liked the warmth and caring that radiated from Aiden and basked in the chance to know this man as a brother.

Aiden smiled. "I have always been, but then I've always known myself. There was a time when my fear was only ever to be myself with claws and rage, the things of childhood nightmares. Or the creature of light, nearly non-existent and untethered. But I have Danny, and he has loved me in all my forms, so I have gained an appreciation for them."

"But I've never seen or felt myself as what you are reflected in any mirror."

"I believe it's because you haven't been open to it. You've felt yourself trapped." Aiden spun his hand in the air, and two seats appeared, one a chaise lounge and the other a high-backed chair.

Out of thin air.

"Sit, we have time. Right now, our Coimeádaithe wait for us. We can't reverse time, but we can set it in slow motion. And while our Coimeádaithe will not suffer the effects, they will understand and give us time while we talk."

Dailon reached out to touch the brown leather chaise, the surface cool to the touch and firm when he pushed.

"Sit. It's real enough where we are."

Aiden sat and reclined back, his suit stretching across his chest, one leg crossed over the other. He smiled kindly when Dailon finally allowed himself to settle comfortably into the curves of the chaise.

"For years now, you haven't known yourself," Aiden began. "But I question your inability to recognize what has been within you all along. Think back. Did you feel a push, pressure beneath the surface?"

Dailon didn't have to think long. There had been moments when he wanted to see how far he could push someone, an eagerness to test what would happen if—if he whispered a thought to them? If he allowed himself to use the power within his grasp?

Could he reveal their secrets and enjoy the outcome? He had known things even as a child that others had never voiced. Thoughts, memories, and even feelings had come to him. A word or two, and suddenly the path a person would take changed, their earlier desire a thing of the past.

All this time.

"There you are, Dailon. I see you. You've known, but you were unable to identify. While you could not visualize your being, he has been there whispering to you."

Dailon closed his eyes, and this time instead of listening outside of himself, he listened within.

There.

It was there, had been there waiting to be recognized, and with the recognition, it uncurled, sliding and twisting, pushing against the surface, and reaching for existence.

"See him. Feel him. He's been waiting too long. Release him."

Dailon threw his head back and roared.

CHAPTER EIGHTEEN

Darren locked gazes with Samuel's wide eyes. They'd been on pins and needles waiting since Aiden had swept Dailon away. But now he felt something, and by the expression on Samuel's face, he felt it too.

Dailon needed them.

Darren was nervous. He knew where Aiden and Dailon had gone. His memory had flashed to being trapped in a world he couldn't escape under the power of a monster.

He didn't know if he could ever go there again, return to a place that still gave him nightmares. Yet the only thing he could do, either of them could do, was to be there for Dailon.

Suddenly Aiden appeared, eyes swirling in Sandman to the tenth power mode, hurricane category 5. "Keepers." His voice echoed around them, then calmed when Danny reached out and touched his hand. "Mine Coimeádaí."

"Always," Danny answered.

Aiden visibly took a deep breath and focused on Darren, then Samuel. "You are needed."

"Obviously," Samuel snapped and pointed to the people who had slowed to a near stop around them. "We can't do a concert like this. Cam and Filly haven't even arrived, and I can't call. I have to wonder how far this reaches."

"It doesn't matter. My brother needs you."

"Your brother?" Darren questioned. "So we were right?"

"Baby, of course, we were. We knew. But Dailon needed to learn." Samuel smiled. "Now, if I'm guessing this right, our Sandman is having trouble with this new part of himself?"

Aiden nodded. "I helped him see within, begin the release, but he won't be able to control himself if you're not there for him."

"And this had to happen now?" Darren muttered.

"Darren, life is not predictable, though we wish it to be. Even we can only do so much, contain so much. Life tosses strands into the air, but we can't catch them all. We can only hold a few while others fall through our fingers. We have to pray someone else will be there to help us gather them. We don't design our tapestries alone. Others help to contribute to our stories. Your story is ready to begin."

Darren took a breath. "I don't know if I can do this."

Aiden opened his arms wide. "You can and you will."

"Darren, he needs us, and we need him." Samuel held out his hand. "This isn't Keith. This is Dailon. Our Dailon."

Darren swallowed hard and took hold of Samuel's hand. Then they both placed their hands into Aiden's.

It was dark and cold. The wind was loud, and the cries were shrieks in the air as it whipped around them. Darren didn't want to be here. The memories of years before when he was forced to his knees, unable to move, powerless, threatened to overwhelm him. He couldn't go through that again, not when he'd worked so hard to rise above it. He'd chosen a profession where he had the power to help those who lacked the control to protect themselves. Those who were where he had once been.

And here he was.

Again.

"No, Darren," Samuel shouted above the wind. "You're not alone here. We're here together, and I would never let you be hurt. Neither would Dailon."

How could Samuel believe that when Darren wasn't even sure of it himself? What made a Sandman resist the temptation of so much power? What made them not try to destroy the ones they professed to love?

"Please trust me," Samuel pleaded. "Have faith in us to help him."

Darren felt Samuel's hand press against his, and he opened his fingers to clasp Samuel's smaller hand tightly.

"There you go, baby. We can do this. You and me. Let's go get the other half of my Double Ds."

Darren laughed, regardless of his frayed nerves. Still, he had to give this a chance. Their bond grew daily, the need to be together overwhelming him as it increased.

"Claim me," a voice whispered around them.

Dailon.

"I hear him, too," Samuel said. "Dailon, we're here."

"Keepers. My Coimeádaithe."

Darren shivered. It was Dailon, and then it wasn't. There was a growl that was more animal than man.

"Darren, he knows we're here. He needs to know we're not afraid, that we have come for him," Samuel insisted.

Samuel was steadier than others gave him credit for. It had been Samuel who'd held him at night when he couldn't sleep alone and Samuel who made him laugh when his fear ensnared him.

On days Samuel had to comfort him, he boasted to the others in the pack that he was *Darren's favorite*. But Samuel was more than that. Samuel was his hope and his dream for the future. If Samuel believed in a life for the three of them, then he believed in it, too.

He took a deep breath and reached for faith. "We are here for you, Dailon. Here to claim what is ours."

"Keepers." The voice was louder this time.

Darren pulled Samuel with him as they sought their Sandman.

Samuel knew Darren was terrified, but they had known this moment would come. If not for Aiden, who knew when, and while this wasn't exactly his choice moment, there was no way he was taking a step back.

That Darren was pulling him confirmed they were both ready for this, no matter how afraid Darren was.

They needed Dailon.

They needed each other.

The mist around them lightened, the vapors decreasing in density as they stepped toward the voice calling them.

How did Dailon look? What would they find? Because there was no way that voice was coming from something human.

"I feel him," Darren said.

Samuel did, too. He ached inside to be closer. "I can smell him," he added.

It was a scent that drew him, as if Dailon's body was sending out waves of pheromones to draw his beast out. He felt his canines drop.

"Keep it together, Samuel."

"Can't, Darren. It's too much. I need him. Need you. Now." Samuel sniffed, inhaling the scent of his other mate.

"There," Darren said and pointed.

Though Samuel found it hard to focus with his need roaring in his ears, he nodded in agreement.

There, larger than life, was Dailon. Not the Dailon they knew, but no matter his form, Samuel knew he was theirs.

The creature before them stood tall and enormous, arms long with clawed hands falling to his knees. Green fur covered him, his neck long with a massive head. Yellow eyes with red pupils watched them while a forked tongue slithered through black lips as if tasting the air.

It was a living, breathing nightmare.

But it was Dailon.

And that was all that mattered.

Part of Samuel wanted to reach out and keep Darren calm, but he couldn't. He could only focus on the creature before them, the need to control and take overwhelming.

When neither he nor Darren moved, Dailon stepped back, his hands up as if to shield himself from their view.

"No," Darren said. "No, Dailon. Don't. We are here for you, to protect you and keep you. You are ours."

"I am not human," Dailon worked the words out beyond his twisting tongue.

"No matter what you are, Dailon, you belong to us." Darren held out his hand. "Come to us. We must be your choice, Dailon. Choose us."

Dailon stared at them, his gaze flicking from one to the other. Samuel moved with the intent of going to him but was blocked.

Darren gripped his arm. "Let him choose, Samuel. He has to believe in us as much as we have to believe in him."

Samuel turned, ready to argue, but froze when he saw Darren reaching to open his jacket and letting it fall from his muscular body. Then he took off his shoes. Next, he unbuttoned his shirt and peeled it away from his skin, moistened with a light sheen of sweat.

Darren's brown skin was magnificent and made Samuel's mouth water with a need to taste. Blood-hunger thrummed through his body. His beast wanted Dailon, but he would also take Darren, worship every bit of his skin.

"Calm, Samuel. Calm," Darren soothed. "Take off your clothes. Let him see you, your need to have him."

It was hard not to keep watching as Darren revealed more of his flesh, but Samuel turned to Dailon, whose clawed hands opened and closed as if he were struggling with himself. He looked at Darren with hunger and need, then glanced at

Samuel with hope.

There you are, Dailon. Darren was right.

Samuel reached for his clothes, pushing off one sandal and then the next. Then he worked on tugging his jeans over his legs and smiled when Dailon gasped.

Dailon obviously loved Samuel's cock, even in his current form. Smiling to himself, Samuel pulled his dick out and slid his hand down the length.

"You want to taste me, Dailon?"

Dailon nodded quickly and dropped to his knees in front of Samuel, mouth open and forked tongue reaching out to taste.

The view made Samuel shiver, but he couldn't wait to shove himself inside Dailon's throat. Placing his hands on the pointed ears, he sank between Dailon's lips and fucked.

"Yes, so good. So very good, Dailon. I like the tongue. Use it on my balls," Samuel demanded.

Dailon huffed, but he gave Samuel what he wanted.

"Yes, just like that." Samuel moaned when Darren wrapped his arms around him from behind and slide his heavy dick between his ass cheeks. He rammed himself into Dailon's throat, crying out when Darren pinched his nipples.

"Don't come, Samuel. We are both claiming him," Darren said. "You want that, Dailon? Want our dicks in your ass, sharing our blood. Want us to fill you up with our seed."

Dailon nodded, his yellow gaze on Darren, shining with hope while his lips stretched wide around Samuel's dick.

"We need your words," Samuel said.

"You need to pull your dick out of his throat so we can hear him ask." Darren chuckled as he slid one of his big hands underneath Samuel's sack.

"But this is so good," he whined. "I don't want to."

"And there's my favorite, taking advantage. We'll make sure Dailon sucks you down again, but we have people waiting, and you have a concert. But first, we need to fill up our Sandman's sweet ass, don't we, Dailon?"

"Sometimes you can be so dirty, Darren. The way you switch back and forth drives me crazy," Samuel moaned but pinched Dailon's jaw to pull himself out.

The moment Samuel removed his dick and the forked tongue released him, Dailon shifted.

A beautifully naked human Dailon knelt before them, his hands on their thighs and his heart in his eyes. "Take me, my Keepers, my lovers. My Coimeádaithe. I am yours. Show me that I belong to you both."

Darren smiled when Dailon knelt before them, phenomenal in his supplication. He was theirs the moment they had been together that first night. He would be theirs for a lifetime.

"You are beautiful, Dailon. We know how strong you are, how much you need to control every aspect of your life, but there are times when you must give up that control and allow us to care for you. Thank you for trusting us."

Dailon's eyes were wet as he gazed up at them.

Darren reached forward and traced one of the tears that fell. "Your mothers were right to trust us. Believe them as we believe you."

"I'm a monster," Dailon whispered before letting his head fall into Darren's palm.

"Never to us," Darren said, taking Dailon's hands in his and tugging him to stand.

"We need a bed." Samuel's hungry gaze flowed over them both.

"Wow," Darren said when Dailon led them to the four-poster California King with ornate antiqued framing, a show-piece he could picture Dailon stretched across at their mercy.

If they showed any mercy.

He pushed Dailon gently against the bed. "There you go, baby."

"Baby?" Dailon repeated.

"Yes, ours. Don't worry. We know how magnificently dominant you can be, but this is for you. We want to take care of you this time. So let us," Darren urged, sliding his hands over Dailon's bronzed skin.

Dailon was all smooth lines and delicious curves just waiting to be tasted, teased. Darren reached and plucked Dailon's nipple, drinking in the sound of his husky gasp.

"Do you have any idea how amazing you two look together?" Samuel growled. "I can barely hold on. I want what Darren wants, to care for you, but I'm so close to breaking down and shoving my dick in your ass."

Dailon nodded helplessly. Darren slid a hand to Dailon's waiting cock and tugged, squeezing out a bead of precum that he swiped with his tongue.

"More, Darren. I need your throat," Dailon pleaded.

Darren gasped against the crown of Dailon's dick and licked again, laughing when his lover reached up to drag him closer.

Darren opened, sliding his mouth along Dailon's length. Then he pulled back, not giving in to Dailon's demands. "Samuel, climb over him. Feed him your cock."

Dailon growled, "I give the commands."

"Not this time, Dailon, not if you want us to claim you. You have to submit. Don't misunderstand, darling. We love when you take over and dictate your dirty wishes. I take liberties in the shower thinking of the tender bruises I've worn on my ass from your hand. And Samuel tied up by you is a thing of beauty. But now? Now, it's our turn."

Darren smiled as Samuel quickly stripped, overeager to follow his orders.

"There you are, Samuel. Yours for the taking." Darren

twisted Dailon's weeping cock, using the slick to draw out the feeling with his fist. "Open up, Dailon. Be a good boy."

"I'll show you a—" was all Dailon managed before Samuel silenced him with his dick.

Samuel fell over Dailon and fucked his mouth hard and fast. "Yes, wider. Wider, Dailon. So good. Gonna come down your throat. Suck me good, baby."

Darren bent to take Dailon in his mouth again, savoring his flavor. Dailon's muffled grunts as Samuel pressed forward made Darren's dick point north. He pushed Dailon's legs apart and slid a wet finger into Dailon's puckered hole.

"He's squeezing my dick with his throat. I'm not going to last much longer. Shove a finger in my ass, Darren. So ready," Samuel groaned.

One hand thrusting in Samuel's ass, the other in Dailon's, Darren wrapped his mouth around Dailon's pulsing dick. The three of them became a writhing, twisting mess.

"There it is. Oh, yes. Yes. So good. I can't wait, Darren. I know I said I could, but I can't. I have to drink him now. Please let me. Please." Samuel whimpered.

Though Darren couldn't see the fangs he knew must have dropped, he could hear the huskiness of Samuel's voice.

"I want to see, Samuel. Let me see you do it, then it will be my turn."

"Yes," Samuel hissed, then his head flew back as he exploded.

"Swallow it—all of it, Dailon. There you go. Yes, lick it clean. Lick it and get every drop."

The sound Dailon let free was beautifully broken.

"Would you like to come, Dailon?"

"So much, please. Yes, I want it. I want you."

"Then tell Samuel what he wants to hear."

Dailon howled, and Darren knew he was fighting his urge for control.

"This only happens when you let go, Dailon. So give us all of you."

Darren shoved two fingers in Dailon's ass and twisted, hitting his target, and Dailon roared.

Chapter Nineteen

Samuel wanted it all. He could taste the blood on his tongue from nipping it with his teeth. The struggle against falling upon Dailon as if his lover were prey was overwhelming, but Darren was right. This had to be about Dailon asking for what they all knew he needed. Samuel wanted to beg the man, but that wouldn't be right.

"Please, Dailon. I have to have you." Okay, maybe a little begging couldn't hurt, but Darren's smack on his ass stung anyway.

"His choice, Samuel. The Fates know," Darren said as he soothed Samuel's cheek with his palm. "Left a pretty red mark there. Want to see it, Dailon? Want to see my handprint on our boy's ass?"

"You know I do, you shit," Dailon growled.

Darren's laugh was dark, and Samuel was more in love than ever. He'd suspected his gentle giant could get dirty, but this was beyond anything he had anticipated. He was giving Dailon what he needed and not holding back.

Samuel stroked his dick over Dailon's lips to encourage his lover. When Dailon licked his tongue out, Samuel hummed in pleasure.

"I can be whatever you need," Darren said. "Lover, protector, asshole. Anything you need."

Dailon's whimper let Samuel know that Darren was working magic in their lover's ass.

"I've never had this before, had someone give me what I need." Dailon's gaze flicked from Darren to him. "It's always me, has always been me."

"Baby, that's why we're here. You are every wish I've ever had. I'm a bit of a handful, and you know this." Samuel did not need Darren's agreeable grunt just then, but seeing Dailon's grin helped. Instead, he focused on the sexy man beneath him whose veins were pulsing with rich, delicious blood he couldn't wait to savor in greedy gulps.

Control. Control.

He smiled. "You give me what I need, and just like our lover here said, we want to give you what you need."

Dailon's eyes were wet, but acknowledging the unshed tears would not win Samuel any brownie points right then. Instead, he rocked his body over Dailon's. He laughed gently when the professor's eyes rolled back, making his neck arch and revealing the tender skin.

Samuel nearly pounced.

"Wait," Darren murmured.

"No, no more waiting. I've been waiting ever since time began and just hadn't realized it. Please, Samuel. Please claim me." Dailon's voice broke, and he swallowed a sob. "Darren, please claim me."

Samuel didn't hesitate. He fell onto Dailon and grasped his throat with sharp teeth, piercing his skin and releasing the delicious bounty he craved.

Images flashed before him as he drank, seeing the world Dailon knew and didn't. The people he'd met on an endless reel. Eons rushing by and then forgetfulness. A time of loss and pain, then Cliona and Aobhill appeared. Dailon's heart overflowing with love and gratitude. Safety. Then need. More time passed. School. Work. Degrees. Samuel experienced all of it as he swallowed. Then there was Samuel and Darren, and Dailon's feelings of absolute joy and the desire to be kept overwhelming him.

Samuel breathed raggedly and licked the spot where he drank, healing the flow. He opened his eyes, his vision blurred by emotion. "You are so yummy. The best dessert. Open up."

Dailon smiled, and his eyes were bright, the blue and gray dancing and swirling, and Samuel's heart swelled with the need to protect and love.

Dailon's mouth was soft and wet, the suction tight when he wrapped his lips around Samuel's girth once again. This time Samuel didn't try to prolong his need. He exploded over Dailon's tongue, rocking back and forth as he emptied himself. Then he hopped off and spun around so Dailon could slide his hand over Darren's handprint.

"It's lovely, Darren. You did this." Dailon said in awe.

"I did, and I liked it. You know he needs it every now and then. I just didn't know how much I would enjoy it until you." Darren laughed. "You showed us what we needed, what could be a part of our relationship and keep the world safe from a naughty Samuel Tolliver."

Samuel shook his head and reached up to offer his lips to Darren, who kissed him tenderly.

Dailon had felt Samuel's claiming click into place and was anxious for the next. "Darren?"

Darren placed his hand, still warm from Samuel's ass, against Dailon's cheek. "Yes, baby."

Dailon settled his chin into the curve of Darren's palm. "Claim me."

"With every part of me, Dailon," Darren whispered.

Samuel lay beside him, drawing circles over his skin. Dailon was nervous. He'd submitted to one of his lovers. Now was the time for the other.

Am I ready for this? Yes, I am. I need them both, not just one but both together. My Keepers.

Before he could go too deep into his head, he moaned when Darren's large frame aligned over him, Darren's crotch against his and warm skin lending heat.

"You are so beautiful, Dailon. I was afraid of this, of you. I feared my destiny, but with Samuel and with you, I know this is where I want to be," Darren said. "I want to be your Coimeádaí. I want to love you and protect you, keep you whole. I don't want you threatening to disappear or for your gifts to leave the world or for you to submit to your inner being and allow it free rein over your soul. I want to be here for you."

The words lodged inside Dailon, wrapping themselves around his heart and buttressing his soul. The creature within settled, as if it knew this was the final piece in the puzzle of their lives.

"This will be different for you, Darren. Your life will never be the same. You will change. You will know more, be more. Your years will lengthen to match mine, and the only sanctuary you may find is that of the pack. I know myself now. I am without end, and you may be that as well. Are you prepared to live a life of eternity with me? Are you prepared to keep me always?"

Dailon feared the answer, but it was not a question he asked lightly. Aiden was right to warn him so that he could be honest with Darren, go in with eyes wide open. Darren had to know what he was risking.

"You will see as I do. Hear as I do. Samuel, as a preternatural creature, will have some defense against this. You are my conduit, my balance. You will know when I am at the edge of darkness and have the power to draw me back. Your soul is my tether, my binding to this world."

"Dailon—"

"Darren, I have to be sure. I can't let you give up who you are and not warn you of what you could become. Your family. Your career. Your life as you know it. It will all change eventually."

"I know, Dailon. I talked with Aiden and Danny." Darren kissed him, dipping his tongue in. "You're not asking me for anything I'm not already willing to give. I know my life will be different, but that's what I want. I thought moving to a new city and opening an office was the difference I needed. It wasn't. It's always been you, baby. I just needed you to finally be here. So no, I'm not going anywhere. Here is where I want to stay. Beside you is where I need to be. Bring on eternity. With you and Samuel there, it will be awesome."

"Are you sure?" Dailon said with hope beating at his heart.

Darren didn't hesitate. "I'm more confident of this than of anything else in my life. So yes, my Sandman, allow me to claim you."

Dailon sighed. "Well, if you must," he teased but couldn't help his tears or the slight tremble in his body.

Dailon was the one afraid. What if Darren couldn't do this? Had he ever drunk from another person? Hell, Dailon had never envisioned it for himself. And now here he was, neck stretched, toes taut, fists at his side, eyes closed while he waited.

"Let me help you, Darren." Samuel, using a claw, tore a gash in Dailon's neck. "There you are. Drink."

Again, Darren didn't hesitate. Instead, he immediately licked once, then twice, then latched on until he was drinking from Dailon's neck.

Dailon could almost come from the suction Darren applied. He keened and wrapped himself around Darren. His heart was racing, the beat so loud he could hear the rhythm of it in his chest. But he needed more, needed it sharper, harder. He needed to be owned.

"What do you need, Dailon?" Samuel asked while driving him crazy with light touches everywhere not covered by Darren's larger body.

"To be claimed by both of you, by Darren," Dailon

growled.

Darren lifted his head, his lips shiny with blood. "Yes." He smiled as his fingers returned to Dailon's ass, stretching and softening his hole, opening him.

Dailon groaned, knowing no matter how many fingers Darren shoved in there, it wouldn't fully ready him for Darren's girth. But he wanted it now. He wanted Darren's dick stretching him, pummeling his prostate while his lips sucked at his throat. He needed Samuel's touch, too. "Now. Please, Darren. Samuel. Now."

And he was suddenly filled without hesitation, Darren's thick rod piercing his body. Then teeth clamped around his throat, the pulling sensation of his blood taken driving him crazy. And touches. Pinches. Hands stretching his legs to help him accommodate the size of Darren's body as he thrust inside.

Dailon stretched his neck back to give them more, to submit. Darren surged into him again and again until he was pressed against the headboard.

"More, please, Darren. Please."

Instead, Darren pulled out. Dailon started to complain because of the sudden emptiness when he wasn't ready, wasn't fulfilled. Then Darren flipped him onto his belly, gripped his ass hard enough to cause bruises, dragged him back, and filled him up again.

Then Darren drank from him once more.

There would be more bruises—lovely bruises everywhere. Dailon opened his eyes and found himself gazing down into Samuel's green ones.

The little demon smiled wickedly before Dailon felt his ass almost split in two as the head of Samuel's cock entered beside Darren.

"You . . . fucker . . ." Dailon gasped.

Samuel smiled. "Fucking you, Dailon. Loving it, too. Kiss

me."

They became a writhing mass of hot, sweaty bodies, fucking, taking. Dailon's cock slid up and down Samuel's slick belly, receiving the added stimulation he craved. When Samuel bit his tongue, he felt his sphincter tighten as his orgasm exploded. Then Samuel roared, and Darren shouted. Together, they floated in bliss, bodies shivering, the sweet stickiness of seed wrapping them together in one enormous ball of ecstasy.

"Thank you," Dailon whispered when he could breathe again. He knew he was crying, but he refused to care. He was claimed. He would be kept.

I am loved.

CHAPTER TWENTY

Darren stood with Dailon, his arm wrapped around Dailon's shoulder as they watched Samuel approach the stage.

Settled. It was a good feeling. Was this what being the Coimeádaí of a Sandman felt like? Light and joyous, buoyant? Darren felt different, new, and happy.

He could wait to see where this new life led them.

There were ways Dailon had envisioned his life, but he'd never dreamed his life would be with two beautiful men—one a mythical being who challenged him daily, which he loved, and the other his deep thinker, attempting to plan every moment.

They had helped him truly discover what lay beneath. He'd accepted long ago there was a part of him that loved life dark and twisty. He craved control and bending things to his will. In the past, that had fulfilled him. Now, it would be Samuel's soft smile when he turned to him in the morning or challenging Darren to a game of timed Sudoku and losing.

Dailon never lost.

And yet, the prospect of giving up control and accepting punishment didn't frighten him with his men. The dominance Darren and Samuel had shown earlier assured him his Keepers would not disappoint him. In fact, he felt quite certain they cared deeply. When they had finally allowed him to come, he had seen stars.

They had given him a part of himself he never knew existed.

Were there signs? Clues? A nudge to my psyche?

Questioning this was laughable.

Dailon wasn't blind to there being moments he couldn't recall, times when he'd been left confused. Dark times where he found himself dreaming of other people, other lives.

And now?

Now nothing remained hidden. Dailon was completely and utterly open to himself and to his men.

They accepted him.

"What are you thinking about?" Darren asked.

"Life. You. The otherworldly creature of ours dancing like mercury on stage."

While Samuel's family knew the wings sprouting from his back were authentic, the audience listening to Samuel's angelic voice did not.

The brightly colored incandescent appendages slowly fluttered as Samuel wiggled about the stage. Filly and Cam accompanied him on drums and bass guitar.

They were magical together, the sinuous way they glided, capturing the attention of every soul in the garden. Conner and his wolves stood on the periphery, ever watchful. Though there hadn't been any sign of trouble since the shooting, the fear that something could happen at any time was still a concern.

Darren drew Dailon closer, and he welcomed the embrace. He placed his head on Darren's shoulder, loving when Darren kissed his temple gently.

"They have no idea," Dailon said as he took in the rapt faces watching Samuel and his band members.

"No, they think the reason he glows is makeup, and the fact he seems to fly is some type of wire set up."

"The human mind is funny that way. It tries to protect itself from things it doesn't understand. They easily deny what is right before their eyes," Dailon laughed.

"But that is how preternatural creatures have remained hidden for eons," Darren whispered.

"True," Dailon agreed.

"You realize you said human. Is that a sign?"

"More a confirmation," Dailon answered. "I know who I am. I know the creature within. Perhaps I always have. In the past, I questioned how to connect or even accept. Now I am ready to know more."

"To explore?"

"Yes, Darren. I am. I think these many years I needed to feel safe to discover my true self."

"And you feel that now? Safe?" There was a thread of hope embedded in Darren's voice.

Dailon refused to let his lover doubt what they shared. "I do. I feel safe with you both. The three of us together are good for one another."

"Yes, we are. That man on stage defying his family by showing his true self needs us now and always."

As if he heard them, Samuel winked and spread his wings before taking his mike in hand. His body glowing with his power, he lifted his chin toward Dailon and Darren, and heads in the crowd turned to see who he indicated.

"What's he up to?" Darren asked with apprehension.

Dailon had learned quickly to expect the unexpected when loving Samuel, their unpredictable one. Yet it was Samuel who gave them balance.

"I'm never certain, but I'm always interested," he replied.

Need radiating from Darren was enough to stir Dailon's interest as well.

"You are not alone in that interest," Darren agreed.

"So, everyone," Samuel called from the stage. "I know you're here for a cause, and it's one close to our hearts. Homeless youth without a safe place is why we're here. Yes, you came to hear us play, see our tricks, and surprisingly, my bandmates decided to support us as well. But not just them, my lovers, too." Samuel pointed at the two of them, blowing each a kiss.

"You know, it's funny. You start life kind of lost, hoping to find your way. You're looking for support, for love, a place to call home. Safety. We're all looking for a safe place." Samuel winked at them.

"He was listening," Dailon said.

"He's always listening," Darren confirmed.

Samuel looked directly at them from his place on stage. "And then in walks your future. Suddenly you not only have everything you dreamed of, but you have what you never realized you needed. Your secrets are laid bare even for yourself." He spun then and ran his hand over his ass.

Darren's inhale mirrored Dailon's. They both knew Samuel was pointing out the location of the red handprint marking his round ass. Darren's palm. The leather pants did nothing to hide what they knew was there.

Dailon's need grew stronger, the desire to take riding him hard. Before he could act, Darren squeezed his shoulder tightly.

"No. Listen," Darren whispered in his ear. "Let's wait for later. There will be time."

Samuel rotated his hips like the bad boy he was, and Filly strode over, pants with so many holes they should have been illegal. Filly smacked Samuel's ass playfully, and the crowd ate it up.

"Oh, yeah, baby. But I love it so much better when it's my Double Ds giving it to me. Safe. I'm safe with them. They're my home."

And then Samuel signaled for the music and began singing to Darren and Dailon.

Can you dream love?

I did.

Can you make those dreams come true?

I have.

I closed my eyes and wished upon a shooting star, and then I found you.

And you.

And now love is no longer just a dream.

Even if we are living in one.

Even if you sprinkle your dust, and I close my eyes, my heart will still find you.

And you.

We will always find each other.

Because we're here

Because you're here

And the love I dreamed is real.

"He's pointing at us again," Dailon said.

"Yes." Darren smiled.

Each time Samuel sang *And you*, he pointed at Darren, then Dailon. The audience followed his gaze, some looking on with shock, others not bothered by the polyamorous love affair revealed before them.

"Only makes me want him more."

"Without a doubt," Darren agreed.

Samuel rose into the air and fluttered his wings. In moments, he stood before the two of them, repeating the final words of the song. "And the love I dreamed is real." His eyes were wet with tears, but his glossy lips bowed into a lovely smile.

Too inviting for Dailon to resist—he bent to kiss Samuel, licking his tongue against the warm flesh for entry. After he'd had a taste, it was Darren's turn with Samuel. His kiss was longer and more heated, and Samuel's skin flushed after it ended.

The applause around them was loud, but not nearly as

loud as the beating of their hearts while they held each other close.

After the concert, Samuel followed Cam and Filly to their hotel room to spend more time with them before they headed for the airport.

"Well, that went well," Cam said as he gathered his bags, handing the heaviest of them over to Filly, who took it without pause. Then he wrapped his arm around Filly's waist. "Thank you, love."

And these two insist they aren't in a relationship. Samuel totally got why it was difficult for anyone witnessing their behavior to believe it. Eventually, one or both would figure out they belonged together. When that happened, the fireworks would be impressive.

When Cam and Filly finished checking out, they headed out the front door.

"You know, I'm surprised the guys let you out of their sight," Cam said.

"Well, they really didn't." Samuel checked back and forth. The road was clear. He wanted to get Cam and Filly back to the airport and then gather his guys as quickly as possible. He wasn't certain Cam was finished interrogating Dailon, and he'd rather skip that for now. Instead, he'd wait with them for their ride and get them on their way. Then he'd collect his guys and head home for some more quality time. He might just get a spanking for leaving without telling them, but spankings were not a bad thing at all. He liked them.

"Samuel Tolliver, you sneaky little bitch, are you using us to get your kink on?" Cam whispered in a dramatic tone.

"What?" Samuel asked.

"You know one of your Daddies is going to spank that ass of yours for leaving without telling them where you went."

Filly snorted and nodded his agreement.

"No, I just don't want the two of you fighting over precious little me. I mean, I am almost perfect. I'm sure I've played a role in a hot fantasy of yours a time or two."

"As if!" Cam shouted.

Filly laughed out loud.

"Oh, and you, too, Filly." Samuel laughed when Filly elbowed him none too gently.

"Quit that shit out before you give Cam a heart attack," Filly groused. "I'm all yours, Cam. Promise."

He's so pretty when he rolls his eyes like that.

Samuel was tempted to poke at Cam more, but now wasn't the time. They needed to get to their flight, and he had to get back to his Double Ds.

"Well, let's get you both out of here and on your way so I can get back before they realize I'm gone. I could drive you there."

"Oh, no," Filly said. "No, we'll take the Uber. We'll get our stuff from your place and head back to the airport. You keep practicing, and you can drive when you come out to the coast."

Okay, so a couple of cars got in the way along with a scooter. No one died. No big deal.

"Fine, I'll be ready. Here's your ride." He gave them both a kiss with a tight hug. He really loved them both. They were the brothers he'd always wanted. He would miss them, but six months would pass quickly.

"Okay, baby. That's enough," Cam said. "We'll be back together in a few months after our hiatus. Keep writing. Send us ideas. Hm. Maybe send us pictures, too. Darren looks good fresh out of the pool. Does he have anything pink?"

"Go, go now," Samuel waved them off as they both got into the Uber that ferried them away.

Samuel turned and nearly walked into a person by surprise.

"What are you doing out here?" he asked.

The pinch of a needle was fast, and Samuel's spill into darkness even faster.

Chapter Twenty-one

Samuel's head hurt like drums and cymbals and all kinds of loud instruments had decided to create a band between his ears. And he couldn't see.

Am I blind?

He blinked and knew his eyes were open, but there wasn't any light, so he still couldn't see anything. He also realized something was stuffed in his mouth, and his hands were bound.

"What do we do with him when he wakes up?"

He heard a harsh whisper in the darkness. He detected fear in the tone as well. So whoever the hell had drugged him wasn't quite sure of their next steps. He could work with that.

Is this the person who tried to kill me?

Weeks had gone by since the shooting with nothing, and here he was, unable to move, barely enough strength to shift.

Where am I?

"We show him how good life can be with you, baby brother. We make him forget all about those two guys. That's the only reason he hasn't called you. He lost his focus. Now, we can help him see you again."

Again? So I've seen the person before. And that bitch. Kate. Karen. Shit. What was her name? Barbara.

Right before he'd been struck by a needle, he'd seen Barbara. She'd said something, but he couldn't remember what. Had she even been speaking to him? It must have been meant for the other person.

What do they call it on detective shows? Accomplice.

Barbara had an accomplice, and this person, who Samuel supposedly knew, was her brother. He had to remember this so he could tell someone else. His Double Ds were probably royally pissed off if they even noticed he was gone.

"I never thought you would pull this off, Barbie."

"I told you I would. You almost had him once. He was yours, and I wasn't going to let Professor Dickhead have him or his muscle-bound bestie. He's yours."

"But Mom and Dad—"

"Didn't know what to do when you used a paring knife during Thanksgiving dinner to open your wrists. They just wanted you to live. I knew what you needed, who you needed. Even though there's something wrong with the family, something strange about them all, I want you to be happy. I don't know what it is. Magic? Whatever he made you drink or do, you couldn't get him out of your system. I don't know the spell he cast, but it broke my heart to hear you cry for him. Now we have him, and we'll never let him go. No more nightmares for you."

There was an icy brush of fingers over his cheek, then cracked warm lips scratched against his. He wanted to fight, to push the person away, but he was too weak.

"There weren't any spells, Barbie. Just him. Only him. Thank you. He's beautiful. He was always beautiful. He loved me. I know he did."

Lies. Samuel never loved anyone before Darren and Dailon. He fucked, and he played. And maybe it was the playing that had come back to bite him in the ass. Perhaps if he'd considered the feelings of those he'd trampled in his need to enjoy their energy, to prey on them, he wouldn't have found himself bound.

When he got out of this, he'd be a better person. With Darren and Dailon, he already was. The energy they shared sustained him. What would happen if he couldn't be with them again? What if Barbara and her brother took him somewhere he couldn't be found?

What if I'm lost forever?

If he'd trained with his father and grandfather, he could probably have done some kung fu jujitsu kind of deal and saved himself. Pulled a knife out of some secret spot next to his cock, like Kristoff probably had. But right then, he could barely think.

"Okay, I'll wait and pretend to look with the others, throw them off," Barbara said. "You stay here with him, but don't let him go. If he looks like he's going to get up again, give him another shot."

"But what if it hurts him?"

"It took enough drugs to take down a horse to get him to pass out. I'm not worried, baby. You want to keep him or not? Me, I can't see why you want him. He only cares about himself. I've been in classes with him for four semesters, and he hasn't changed. So many projects together, and the little asshole barely remembers my name."

"I don't know, Barbie. I don't know."

"Shh, it's okay, sweetheart. No more tears, okay. You do what you need. Take what you need to feel better. It's your turn to be happy."

"The therapist said to find the source of my pain, to talk it out."

"That asshole's dead now. We don't need to think about him anymore. Samuel's what you needed. That's what will help."

"We shouldn't have killed him."

"*We* didn't. I did. You don't have to worry about any of this. I did what I've always done, take care of you. Now, I have to get out and return, or they may suspect something. Be the sweet simpleton everyone loves. As for you, I can see you want to do more than touch him. Can you wait until we get him home? That way, you can be alone. You can take care of him there, okay?"

"Yes, Barbie."

The hand never stopped touching and stroking almost incessantly.

"Paul?"

"Yes, Barbie?"

"If you want to make him bleed, you can." There was a slight edge to Barbie's voice. "I understand, okay. Sometimes people have to bleed to know how much they're loved. "

There was a clicking sound, then a door shut. Were they in a vehicle? Was that how they'd picked him up off the street?

Samuel tried reaching out to Dailon and Darren, but the more he tried, the more painful his headache became. Then came the nausea.

"Samuel, it's okay. All right. I won't let her hurt you. I know she wants you to feel what I've gone through without you for the last few years. She doesn't understand, you know. I had to feel like I was dying, almost die really, to appreciate the light you bring to my life. I was wrong to leave you. Wrong to let them take me away. I'm here now, and I won't let anyone hurt you, not even Barbie. She loves me, sometimes too much. Having to practically raise me herself sometimes messes with her head, you know?"

There was a rustling sound, then a body was behind Samuel, arms wrapped around him from behind.

"This feels good. You never let me inside you, Samuel. I could be good for you. Can I open your pants a little? Just let me touch you. I just want to touch you. You're so warm."

A wet tongue against Samuel's neck as his leather pants tore at the edge. It wouldn't take much to remove them, since he'd wanted to be ready for his Double Ds the moment they wanted him.

"You taste so good. The oil on your skin is fruity. You make me hungry." Paul giggled and nibbled at his neck.

Strong arms pulled him tighter against a muscular frame.

"I'm bigger now. Barbie said that would help. She said you needed someone stronger. Am I strong enough for you now, Samuel?"

A hand gripped his ass and pulled him close.

"I've waited so long to feel you, to have you. Can I have you, Samuel?"

Samuel tried to shake his head. He wanted to attack, but he was weak, and his arms were bound. He couldn't fight the hand at his waist, the fingers sliding along the curve of his ass, or the fingers that shoved roughly into his hole.

"Not yet, Barbie said. I'm just going to rock against you like this. I could come against your ass with your tightness wrapped around my fingers. Are those tears, Samuel? No, baby, don't cry. Wait. Wait until I get you home. That's when all the tears can come. I'll help you wipe them. I'm here for you. You're my gift. I'll take care of you."

Paul kissed the back of Samuel's neck, licking before biting hard enough to break then skin.

"You taste so good, feel so good." He grunted while shoving himself against Samuel, then roared with his release. "That was nice, Samuel. I want to do it again. Can I hold your dick?" Paul laughed, the sound ugly and twisted. "It's not like you can say no. You can never say no again, can you, Samuel?"

"Where is he," Darren growled and worried.

There were so many people milling about, and Samuel was nowhere to be seen. He'd walked backstage with Cam and Filly after signing autographs and talking about the reason they were all here, to help homeless gay youth. It was a cause Darren could get behind. Many of his friends were not nearly as lucky as him when it came to having a family who supported them.

And now, here he stood, looking around for the sweet filling to their cookie sandwich.

"I don't know. Since the claiming, I've been able to recognize an awareness belonging to both of you. Right now? I feel an emptiness where Samuel's presence should be."

And that was beyond worrisome. Darren hated to consider the worst. Immediately his thoughts went to a shattered car window. They'd found nothing so far. Was Conner right, and they should have been more vigilant? This event was the first large public adventure they'd attended together. Before the concert, they had done a movie here, a dinner there, occasionally spending their nights together wrapped in each other's arms. Samuel had promised only the night before that he would be careful, even though he felt there was nothing to worry about.

That Dailon couldn't feel Samuel wasn't what Darren wanted to hear. If anything, their connection should be growing stronger since they'd completed the bonding. Adding to that the concern for Samuel's safety since the shooting only weeks ago, the need to contact Conner to begin looking for their lover became overwhelming.

He continued to search the crowd while he pulled out his phone to text Conner. Everyone looked at ease, talking about the project and the end results. Those who had promised to contribute funds were in the process of leaving. Darren hated to be the one to disrupt the newfound possibilities for the homeless kids, but Samuel was his chief concern.

He looked at Dailon, who was deep in thought.

"I am searching," Dailon said. "I'm looking through the psyche of those around us. Attempting to see if something is hidden beneath the surface." His eyes changed and swirled as he used his power.

Darren spotted Aiden heading their way, the crowd

around him freezing as he passed.

"What's wrong," Aiden shouted. "I can feel your energy."

"Samuel's missing," Darren answered while Dailon continued to focus. "I'm contacting Conner."

"Shit," Aiden replied as his eyes clouded until the pupils were mercury and cobalt, sliding over and under.

Both men were deep in concentration while the people around them moved as if the air was thick and heavy, arms and limbs barely moving.

Conner, though, blazed his way through, his wolves following in his wake, alert and ready. "Tell me what you know."

Darren told them what little he knew while the two Sandmen continued their search. Samuel had come to them after working the crowd. He'd kissed them both, then he and his bandmates had disappeared backstage. Almost an hour had passed since then. Thinking they were packing, he and Dailon hadn't worried at first. However, after messaging and calling and still no Samuel, Dailon had mentioned he couldn't sense their mate.

"Shit, that boy. He knows better," Conner growled. He thrust his fingers into his hair as if he wanted to tear out the very strands. Shaking his head, he turned to his wolves. "Shift and search for my brat. Say nothing of this to his mother. She will skin me, pelt and all. Go."

The four with Conner nodded and dropped to the floor, the shift upon them quickly. Then a black, a burnished orange, and two gray wolves took off. Conner turned back to the Sandmen. "How long have they been like this? Have they spoken?"

"Not long before your arrived. First, Dailon then Aiden, when he learned of Samuel missing."

Conner nodded while he removed his weapon. "My wolves will keep to the perimeter, searching for signs of a struggle. They are familiar with Samuel's scent and will alert us should they find anything. Dailon, if he is anything like Aiden, will be sifting through the thoughts of those around us."

Suddenly both men took a deep breath and looked toward the edge of the garden. Then they ran.

"Follow them," Conner shouted as he took off after Dailon and Aiden.

Darren kept up as well as he could, a human following a wolf who chased two Sandmen. While Dailon and Aiden appeared to be human, the way they moved was supernatural. They sped past the waning crowd until they stood before a woman, who was suddenly frozen in place.

He recognized her as one of Samuel's study group members. She looked at them all defiantly. Gone was the sweet cherub face, the quiet and hopeful student vying for attention. Barbara faced them as if prepared for battle.

She obviously knew something, and with the way the wolves surrounded her as they joined the Sandmen, they weren't fooled by the innocence she'd projected when she'd arrived on the grounds.

"Barbara, where is Samuel?" he asked.

"As if I would tell you," she spat out with so much venom and hate. "You all think you're so great. Think you can get away with anything. Hurt anyone. Well, Samuel belongs to my brother now. There's no way I'm telling you anything."

"Oh, you're going to tell us, little girl." Samuel's mother approached like an avenging angel, and the way she bore down on Barbara was a thing of beauty.

Briefly, Darren wondered if any of the onlookers left behind had noticed the way the weather had changed to match Shelly's ire or felt the danger of her presence.

"I don't have to say a thing," Barbara stated in a defiant tone. "When I tried to get you to listen to us before, to tell you that we knew my brother hadn't dreamed it all, that he had come here and Samuel had used him and thrown him away, you refused to believe us. You tried to make us think it wasn't real, that nothing had happened. But it did. I knew it was true. All of it. Paul remembered, and he told me. We tried to get him help, tried to get him past this, over Samuel, but your son is like a drug, and Paul was addicted. It's not fair for him to have so much power, for your family to be able to do what you did and not suffer."

Shelly took a deep breath. "I know. We all know how Samuel can be, could be. But he's changed."

Barbara's laugh was a little unhinged, and her eyes were wet with tears. "Changed. Since when? Since he started fucking his boyfriend and Professor Walker? Since he became their bitch? Well, now your changed boy can be Paul's. He deserves to be happy, and no matter how much I hate your asshole son, my brother loves him. Knowing that he would have a chance to be with him is the only thing keeping him alive. He hasn't once tried to kill himself since I promised to give him Samuel, and there's no way in hell I'm changing that. So do whatever you want to do."

The crack of Shelly's fist against Barbara's cheek was loud, but one of the wolves caught the girl when she fell.

"I'm sorry, but he's my son." Shelly turned to the Sandmen. "Aiden and Dailon, find my boy."

Unconscious, Barbara's thoughts would be like a dream, and with that, the Sandmen flowed into her mind. Their eyes wide open and searching, they breathed as one until they gasped. In sync, they turned toward the gate.

"He's in a van," Dailon said. "They knocked him out. He's drugged, and her brother is with him."

"Can you sense Samuel yet?" Darren asked.

"No, my awareness of him is still muted. We'll have to search for him."

"It shouldn't be hard," Connor said.

And it might have been easy to find him if there had been a van in the parking lot, but the only vehicles were cars, SUVs, and a couple of motorcycles.

"Aiden," Connor shouted, "grab your bike. We'll follow. They can't have gotten far."

They were moving, and while Samuel's head was still pounding, he was more lucid than he had been when his world had spun around.

Paul. He remembered him now. He'd tasted his energy and shared some of his own. He'd been reckless and irresponsible and had left the man behind.

But just because I've ignored my past mistakes doesn't necessarily mean they forget me.

He could smell Paul's semen on him, feel the air on his skin where the man had touched and fondled him. The man hadn't raped him, but there was a good chance it was going to happen if he didn't get his ass out of the van.

He tried calling to Dailon again, but this time he felt a pulse, where so many tries earlier had only resulted in sharp pain.

Samuel

Samuel gasped. He felt him, felt his Sandman. He was coming for him, and if he was, Darren wouldn't be too far behind.

"Once I get us home, I'll take care of you, okay? Barbie will meet us later. She said she would have to distract them. That way, I could get you to safety. She'll come later. My sister is so smart. Fooled you." Paul just kept talking. "You had no idea who she was. She'll be here later." The crazy man's voice was off-kilter, his driving erratic as he spun the wheel this way and that. "I'm sorry about the bumps. I'd let you sit up, but I can't. I need to give you more medicine, too. I have more. Soon. Then we can play some more, okay?"

"Paul," Samuel whispered. He'd managed to spit out the gag, but his throat was dry, and his stomach felt nauseous.

What did they give me?

"Shut up! You shut up! I need to give you more medicine. But I can't right now, so don't talk, okay? I don't want to hurt you. I want to love you."

"You can't do this."

"Shit. I said shut up, Samuel."

The vehicle swerved to the right, and Samuel winced when his head slammed against the corner of a box.

"I will make you. I will make you shut up." Paul stood over Samuel, a metal pipe in his hand. "You see this? If you don't fucking be quiet, I will beat you with this. I want to hit you. I should hit you for making me wait this long to be with you, but I won't. You like being punished, right? Being a good boy. Be a good boy, Samuel, or I will splatter your brains on this floor."

The pipe clattered next to Samuel's head, and he closed his eyes, praying his Double Ds would find him before Paul made good on his promise.

The van continued moving.

CHAPTER TWENTY-TWO

Samuel was cold, chilled to the bone cold, but sweating at the same time. His stomach was swimming, but he wasn't rocking on the floor of the van anymore. There was a blanket wrapped around him, and his body ached.

"Shh. We have you now, baby. You're safe," a voice whispered next to him. Darren.

His lover's strong arms wrapped around his body while a cup was held to his lips.

"Drink this, Samuel." Dailon's voice. "Mrs. Donovan says it should help get you up and flying again. We don't know what was in the needle they used, but if it was strong enough to hurt you, it's cause for worry."

Dailon smelled good. So good.

He was home. Not his home. He was in his childhood room in the large pack dwelling. Again.

"Home," he whispered, but the crackly voice that exited his lips was barely one he recognized. Had he been screaming?

"I know. Soon. I think we both know how much you want to leave, but we have to give your family time to smother you. You've put them through the wringer, okay?" Darren said.

Samuel sipped the liquid from the cup. Tea.

Ugh. Sweat socks.

"What do you mean?" Samuel asked. While the tea was revolting, it had helped to soothe his throat and repair his voice in just a few sips. His cough was lighter as he spoke. "How did I get here? I don't remember anything other than Paul's threats. Rolling around in the van. My head still hurts, too." But not as it had earlier. His skin was hot, too. Scorched, if he had to use a word for it. And he ached. Itched. It was all different, like something he never experienced before.

His tongue felt large in his mouth, the teeth sharper than when he was a wolf.

Did I shift while I was in the van?

But if he had connected with his wolf, wouldn't he have known? Shared thoughts? An awareness of his other? He felt something, but it wasn't his wolf.

"We had no idea, little one." His mother's voice was in awe as she walked into the room.

"None of us did," Conner confirmed.

"We did." Two voices said in unison.

Why were Dailon's mothers here? How long had he been out? He was confused and disoriented. He was also hungry, the need for blood overwhelming.

"Dailon," he growled.

"And there it is. The creature is there. Waiting. It will surpass the wolf in its need to claim its mates, to know their bond has not been broken so newly formed." Aobhill said kindly. "I would suggest we give them the space needed, and then he may recover fully."

Recover fully?

What did he need to recover from?

As he tried to take everyone in, his eyes finally regaining focus, instead of bodies, he saw only light. Different hues. Various degrees of heat. But light alone.

And while that was fearsome, nothing compared to the need to taste and touch. Samuel wanted to devour. A rage heated his skin at not being able to do just that.

"We need to leave now," his grandfather said. "I can sense the energy changing. Cliona and Aobhill, most honored mothers. We are grateful for your presence and your return to the world. We would break bread with you as days of old and hear your stories."

There were too many words and not enough movement.

Samuel wanted to roar, to bathe the room in flames. He wanted his mates.

"We accept, and in an effort to move quickly, we will all leave the room." Aobhill was insistent.

"While I'm not entirely certain what's happening here, I would have to agree." His mother's tone was unsure but encouraging. "I am just grateful to have my son home. Mothers." She waved toward the door.

"Daughter," Cliona and Aobhill chorused.

There were sudden movements, and then Samuel and his mates were alone.

"Mates," Samuel hissed. His tongue slid around sharp blades of fangs, his fingers capped in claws as he pressed into the forgiving surface beneath him.

"Oh, beautiful, beautiful boy. I'm sure Darren and I will both agree we had no idea you kept such an amazing creature within," Dailon said before kissing him.

Gentle fingers caressed Samuel's skin, and the roar building in his belly eased to a hum.

"You are not easy prey, little one, no matter what my mothers thought," Dailon said as he licked at Samuel's throat.

The hum changed to a moan.

"Need," Samuel groaned. His ability to speak in complete sentences had evaporated. He was sensations and feelings, ache and hunger.

"He has no idea, does he?" Darren asked.

"None, but we are here for him. We will feed him and return him to his human form."

Riddles. Samuel didn't want riddles, no mysteries. He stood and was surprisingly looking down on both of his mates. He felt the buffet of wings striking the walls, heard the crashing of furniture, but he ignored it all, driven by his need for his mates.

They were beautiful, his mates. He opened his arms and grabbed his Sandman, bringing him close, wrapping himself around his warmth, and drawing in his scent.

It was his turn to lick and taste, to plunder Dailon's suddenly naked body, drawing claws along his tender flesh.

"Need."

"I know, Samuel," Dailon growled.

The words vibrated against his chest as Dailon stretched, arching into his touch, gasping when he wrapped his clawed fist around Dailon's cock.

"Take. Claim." His words came out scratchy and rough.

Samuel kept his gaze on Darren, his own need reflected in the depths of Darren's blown pupils. He walked forward with Dailon in his arms until they were close enough to touch Darren. "You are mine. Both of you."

Darren nodded. "We are. We always will be."

They were his sun, the light glorious and life-giving, filled with joy and hope. It was love. It was everything he needed and so much more.

Samuel slammed his lips against Darren, and for a second, he wondered why he felt so much bigger. Usually, he was the one looking up, reeling in Darren's tender gaze.

Now? Now he was manhandling a nearly orgasmic Dailon and slipping his tongue around Darren's and pulling him closer.

When he ended the kiss, Darren was breathless, his lips swollen.

Samuel groaned. "So good. More."

"Whatever you need, baby," Darren whispered.

"I need you naked."

Darren laughed. "Yes, sir."

"No."

"No sir?" Darren questioned.

"No. Mate. Say mate. Claim me." Samuel needed to make them understand.

"Mate," Darren repeated and smiled.

That was what Samuel needed to hear. "Good. Strip." He ached for more of Darren's skin.

"Maybe I need foreplay," Darren husked.

"Later. Need to fuck Dailon. Then you. Come all over you. Claim you." Samuel felt more guttural, more animal than he'd ever felt as his wolf. This moment was all about instinct and feeling. Everything else would be too many words.

What he needed mattered.

The feel of his lovers squeezing his cock mattered.

And blood. He needed their blood.

"Blood," he managed to growl.

Dailon shivered and his head fell back, his ass rolling over Samuel's dick. "Keeper." His voice, otherworldly.

The only human left in the room was Darren. He was their balance, the tie that bound them together.

Samuel sank his teeth into Dailon's shoulder and savored the resulting howl. Licking his lips, he lifted his head and stared into Darren's eyes. "Kiss me."

"Shit," Darren said before leaning in and kissing him.

Samuel took over and deepened the kiss, then pulled back. "Good. But you still have clothes on." *Finally*. He could almost feel himself becoming normal.

Darren yanked his shirt off, his eyes glazed over, the taste of his Sandman's blood clearly overwhelming his senses. He toed off his shoes, tore at his pants until they joined the shirt on the floor. Then he stood tall, all golden-brown skin and curves, his dick hard and proud.

Samuel lifted Dailon, carrying him to the bed, licking his shoulder to still the bleeding.

"My treasure," he said as he turned to face Darren. "Come to me."

Darren stepped forward and gasped when Samuel grasped his dick then palmed his ass, his claws sliding along Darren's skin. He tugged and enjoyed the beads of precum that appeared, taking the drops and tasting them before spinning Darren around and slamming him against the wall. He fell to his knees behind Darren, pushed him over at the waist, then split his ass cheeks.

"Put your hands on the wall. Spread your legs. Need you. Have you?" He was just enough human to ask, to restrain himself, but barely.

"Yes, Samuel. Please."

Samuel laughed. "Darren. My Darren." He drilled his face into the warmth of Darren's ass, sinking his tongue deep into his anus and stretching him.

"Fuck. Fuck," Darren shouted. "Baby."

Samuel couldn't help but nip at his mate's skin and rejoiced at the sparkling bits of his blood that appeared. Jewels. Precious stones. He savored the flavor. It was everything.

He dragged Darren to the floor, lifted his ass, and pushed his thighs further apart. He would need the room. He was bigger than he'd ever been, the weighty cock between his legs eager to find its way home in Darren's body. He curved himself over Darren's body, pressing the head of his cock against Darren's slick hole.

"Ready." It was a growl, but it was all he could give.

"Please, Samuel," Darren begged.

That was all he needed. He thrust forward, filleting Darren's ass.

"Oh, Samuel. So fucking big, baby. I've never been this full before."

Samuel locked in, wrapping his wings around them both. "No one will take mine," he roared as he punctuated each word with the thrust of his cock.

Darren fell forward, but Samuel held tight, one hand

grasping Darren's dick. The other pulled Darren's knee away from his body to make more room for his growing member.

"Shit. Shit. Samuel." Darren trembled.

"Take me, mate. All of me." Samuel wanted to be a part of his mate's body and soul.

Darren started mewling, his cheek sliding across the floor. "So much."

"Claiming." Samuel stood, Darren still impaled on the end of his dick. He rocked himself in and out, hard and deep, and sank his teeth into Darren's neck.

When he made it to the bed where Dailon lay with his hand stroking himself, he opened his mouth and hummed in approval as Dailon crawled to him. Dailon, his Sandman, his mate. So strong yet so vulnerable.

"Drink. Feed," he commanded Dailon.

Dailon was on Darren immediately, swallowing at his throat.

When Dailon had his fill, Samuel clawed his throat until blood drizzled down his skin.

"Feed," he told Darren while still thrusting into him.

Darren fell forward into Dailon's arms and placed his mouth at his neck. He held Dailon tight as Samuel fucked him deep and long.

Darren shook but continued to drink, moaning roughly as Samuel thrust faster, extending his wings to envelop all three of them.

Dailon looked up, his Sandman eyes blazing, his hand gently caressing Darren's head as their lover was changed forever.

Then Samuel roared, filling Darren's ass with his seed. Darren shook and trembled, his mouth falling away from Dailon's neck.

For long moments, Samuel held himself still, sealing his essence within Darren's body, completing his claim on body and soul.

The fear of not being able to return, of being lost to them? No. They would fully accept, fully know each other.

Darren slid onto the bed, and Samuel released him before dragging a surprised Dailon to him.

"Open," he whispered before falling on Dailon, pressing himself inside his warmth, thrusting his way home.

He grabbed both of Dailon's legs and wrapped them around his waist. Then he bore down on him as he had Darren. Dailon's mouth was open in a wide *O*, his breath ragged from being taken.

"More, Samuel. My mate. My dragon. More." Dailon shouted.

Dragon.

He pulled Dailon closer and latched on to his neck, sucking more of the rich and heady fluid, savoring the essence.

Dragon.

Vague memories began to flash in his mind. Paul saying how he would go back and kill Dailon and Darren after he stashed him somewhere safe. He would make sure Samuel didn't need them anymore.

His rage had been lightning fast.

Dragon.

He'd opened his mouth to yell, and fire had erupted from the bowels of his belly, incinerating everything around him. Paul had screamed in surprise then veered off the road, the van doors flying open to freedom.

But the dragon hadn't been satisfied. It had destroyed the bindings and hunted down its prey.

Dragon.

As the memories faded, his wings grew less heavy as he continued to pump himself inside Dailon. His vision slowly changed, no longer light but forms.

Dragon.

He erupted once again, but this time in his other mate,

inside Dailon's warmth, fully satisfied that he'd claimed them both. His essence was seated inside them. *Mine*. His treasures.

His alone.

He tightened his arm around Dailon and still had enough strength to drag Darren's weak form next to them. Then his wings settled around them all, and he slept.

Epilogue

"Mr. Samuel?"

The words were a whisper, but Samuel was grateful to hear them. The boy hadn't said much since he'd moved to the shelter they'd built with the money raised during the mini-concert. With the funds still coming in, they had been able to establish not only a safe place for the throwaway kids to live but were also able to provide them ways to secure their independence.

Rainbow Homes helped these kids get on their feet, get an education, and find jobs. They gained confidence and hope. They learned skills. And for some, like this little guy, they were able to find trust.

Samuel had helped with that as a counselor. Maybe meeting Paul, being trapped and forced to face the misery he'd contributed to, was the driving factor he needed to discover his calling.

"Yes, Micah." He smiled down at the boy.

The tow-headed kid would be a beauty someday. For now, he was a scrawny kid with too-wide teeth who jumped at his own shadow. When he'd first arrived, he was hungry. Hiding food and hissing like a lost kitten. He wasn't far from that now, but they'd made progress.

"You said I could help you write a song." Music was the string that helped them to connect.

"I did."

"Well, I couldn't sleep last night, so I wrote some words. Could you look at them? Tell me what you think." His voice had become stronger, his joy at having something to share too great to hide.

"Yes, I can. And your end of the bargain?"

"I did my homework and didn't cuss out the teacher yesterday."

Samuel had heard the boy had slammed the door after walking out of the class, but progress was progress. And Micah *had* eaten the meals they'd offered. Samuel had checked on that, too.

"Good." Samuel moved his seat forward to look at the tablet Micah slid carefully to him.

He glanced at the boy, then down to the words before him. Reading the lyrics, he could almost hear the accompaniment himself. It was sad, speaking of lost dreams and no home, of beatings, and the snipping of butterfly wings.

"Are you crying, Mr. Samuel?" the boy asked.

"Yeah, Micah. I am."

"I'm sorry."

"No reason to be. This is beautiful. I can hear the music. Filly is going to love this."

Watching Micah's face light up made everything worth it.

Was Samuel perfect? No. But he'd become a better person. He was helping to make a difference. He was giving his rainbow boys and girls hope.

Later, Samuel sat in his office, his focus on the door Micah had exited. The boy's steps were a little lighter, his face beaming with a soft smile of wonder as he walked out. Samuel had ensured a snack would be waiting for him in his room.

"So how's my favorite counselor doing today?" Darren asked as he walked in.

"I still have a few classes to go before that title is mine."

"Yes, but you're well on your way. Fortunately for you, being a serial class taker worked out. Put together, you actually had a degree's worth already. Give me a kiss."

Samuel laughed but rounded the desk to happily obey the command. "I'm doing fine. Micah shared song lyrics with me today."

"Did he?"

"Yes."

"And how do you feel about that?"

"Are you counseling me, Attorney Darren Carpenter?"

"No, just checking in." Darren kissed him again.

Suddenly, Samuel's pants were tighter. He licked his lips, hungry for more. Clearing his throat, he said, "I feel like I'm making a difference. Making up for Paul and maybe others."

"You know, Paul was a grown man. He made his choices."

"But how many of those choices were because of me? How many were because he didn't feel loved for who he was? Instead of taking what I could, I should have given him more."

Darren nodded, but then he placed a finger beneath Samuel's chin and lifted it until he could gaze into his eyes. "None of us can change the past, not even our Sandman who's waiting outside for us. The only thing we can do is work on the present to ensure a better future. I love what you're doing here. I love you. That's all that matters." After a quick kiss, he added, "Now, we have a man who will stop the world if we don't get our asses in gear. Let's go."

Samuel smiled and turned to grab his bag. "Where are we going?"

"None of that. Come on."

"So it's a surprise. Ow!"

"Disobedient boys get spankings. Now, move it."

Samuel's dick had other things on its mind now, but Darren was moving like it was his ass on fire. He'd do his best to get what he wanted later, though.

"Yes, Daddy."

Darren laughed as he tugged on Samuel's hand and guided

him out the door.

Dailon watched the two men he loved walk toward him. Samuel, his metaphysical mutt, a wolf, a sprite, and a dragon. Who knew? Certainly not him, but that was fine. He liked this life, the one where he was never bored, where his men kept him on his toes and kept him grounded.

My Keepers.

It bothered him that his mothers had kept such a secret from him, but they had their reasons. Who was he to argue with fairy royalty? He missed them already, but it was long since time for them to return to their lives.

As they said, he was in capable hands.

Cliona and Aobhill had taken Paul's sister with them. They liked her strength and felt it was wasted here in the human world. As for Paul, some things couldn't be helped, but he would be remembered as the catalyst that gave Samuel direction.

Instead of dwelling on the past, Dailon reached into his pocket to caress the matching necklaces he'd created. Dreamcatchers. His token to his mates. Interwoven with the beings Samuel harbored within was a sun to represent Darren. He was the light that guided them and held them all together.

This night, Dailon would ask them to live with him, to share his home and life. They were his Keepers, but he needed to keep them as well. He still taught at the university, Darren worked in Louisville now, and Samuel was a counselor at the Rainbow Home. What could be more perfect?

It was time for them to create their own home. Maybe even with children of their own. Only time would tell.

And he was a Sandman with no more broken dreams. He had all the time in the world.

About the Author

Deja Black had fantasies of men loving men, men who felt strongly, loved hard, and needed a hero. Then one great day she came across a book and discovered the world of m/m writing, encountered others who shared her obsession as much as she did, and found a world where she could not only be accepted for the lives and loves she envisioned, but she could create them too. So why not? Why not take the stories she would write and throw away as a teenager, grow them, dream them, and make them a reality where she could let them live their story, and make them real for someone else? And she did. Now, with the support of her hubby and some intense time management, she is learning to balance her family of two energetic children at home, along with the many students she counsels every day, as well as her passion for writing what she loves to read. Oh, and did you know she has two beautiful frogs now? Life is full of surprises.

Deja is always interested in connecting to new people who also share her love, so please feel free to contact her at:

Facebook: www.facebook.com/deja.black.69

Blog: https://dejablack77.blogspot.com/

Twitter: @DejaBlack69

www.ingramcontent.com/pod-product-compliance
Lightning Source LLC
LaVergne TN
LVHW050630100826
845148LV00011B/1810